"No reason why something can't be both useful and beautiful."

Andrea tracked the scalloped edge of the drop leaf Cal had carved. "This certainly qualifies. You make lovely furniture. I just can't help but wonder why you're doing it in my grandmother's barn."

"Didn't you know? I'm your grandmother's tenant."

Where did you come from, and why are you here? That's what she was really asking. How could this man have made such inroads with her family when she hadn't even known about him? It wasn't any of her business, but anything that affected her grandmother and sister mattered to her, whether she'd been back recently or not.

Most people liked talking about themselves. Cal Burke seemed to be the exception.

MARTA PERRY

has written everything, including Sunday School curriculum, travel articles and magazine stories in twenty years of writing, but she feels she's found her writing home in the stories she writes for the Love Inspired line.

Marta lives in rural Pennsylvania, but she and her husband spend part of each year at their second home in South Carolina. When she's not writing, she's probably visiting her children and her five beautiful grandchildren, traveling, gardening or relaxing with a good book.

Marta loves hearing from readers, and she'll write back with a signed bookmark. Write to her c/o Steeple Hill Books, 233 Broadway, Suite 1001, New York, NY 10279, e-mail her at marta@martaperry.com, or visit her on the Web at www.martaperry.com.

Hide in Plain Sight
Marta Perry

Steeple
Hill®

Published by Steeple Hill Books™

STEEPLE HILL BOOKS

Steeple
Hill®

ISBN-13: 978-0-373-44255-3
ISBN-10:   0-373-44255-6

HIDE IN PLAIN SIGHT

www.SteepleHill.com

Printed in U.S.A.

For everything there is a season, and a time to every purpose under heaven: a time to be born and a time to die; a time to plant and a time to uproot; a time to kill and a time to heal.

—*Ecclesiastes* 3:1–3

This story is dedicated to my gifted editor, Krista Stroever. And, as always, to Brian.

ONE

She had to get to the hospital. Andrea Hampton's fingers tightened on the steering wheel as that call from the Pennsylvania State Police replayed in her mind in an endless loop. Her sister had been struck by a hit-and-run driver while walking along a dark country road— like this one. They didn't know how badly she was injured. Repeated calls to the hospital had netted her only a bland voice saying that Rachel Hampton was undergoing treatment.

Please. Please. She wasn't even sure she believed any longer, but the prayer seemed to come automatically. *Please, if You're there, if You're listening, keep Rachel safe.*

Darkness pressed against the windows, unrelieved except for the reflection of her headlights on the dark macadam and the blur of white pasture fence posts. Amish country, and, once you were off the main routes, there were no lights at night except for the occasional faded yellow of oil lamps from a distant farmhouse.

If she let herself picture Rachel's slight figure, turning, seeing a car barreling toward her... A cold hand closed around her heart.

After all those years she had protected her two younger sisters, Rachel and Caroline were independent now. That was only right. Still, some irrational part of her mind seemed to be saying: *You should have been here.*

A black-and-yellow sign announced a crossroads, and she tapped the brakes lightly as she approached a curve. She glanced at the dashboard clock. Nearly midnight.

She looked up, and a cry tore from her throat. A dark shape ahead of her on the road, an orange reflective triangle gleaming on the back of it... Her mind recognizing an Amish buggy, she slammed on the brakes, wrenching the wheel with all her strength. *Please, please, don't let me hit it—*

The car skidded, fishtailing, and she fought for control. Too late—the rear wheels left the road and plunged down into a ditch, tipping crazily, headlight beams spearing toward the heavens. The air bag deployed, slamming into her. For an instant she couldn't breathe, couldn't think.

As her head began to clear she fought the muffling fabric of the air bag, the seat belt harness digging into her flesh. Panic seared along her nerves, and she struggled to contain it. She wasn't a child, she wasn't trapped—

A door slammed. Voices, running feet, and someone yanked at the passenger door.

"Are you hurt? Can you talk?"

"Yes." She managed to get her face free of the entangling folds. "I think I'm all right, but I can't reach the seat belt."

"Hold on. We'll get you out." A murmured consultation—more than one person, then. The scrape of metal on metal, and the door shrieked in protest as it was lifted.

"The buggy." Her voice came out in a hoarse whisper. "I didn't hit it, did I?"

"No," came a curt male voice, and then a flashlight's beam struck her face, making her blink. "You didn't."

Hands fumbled for the seat belt, tugging. The belt tightened across her chest, she couldn't breathe—and then it released and air flowed into her protesting lungs.

"Take a moment before we try to move you." He was just a dark shadow behind the light. In control. "Be sure nothing's broken."

She wanted to shout at him to pull her free, to get her out of the trap her car had become, but he made sense. She wiggled fingers, toes, ran her hands along her body as much as she could.

"Just tender. Please, get me out." She would not let panic show in her voice, even though the sense of confinement in a small, dark space scraped her nerves raw with the claustrophobia she always hoped she'd overcome. "Please."

Hands gripped her arms, and she clung instinctively to the soft cotton of the man's shirt. Muscles bunched under the fabric. He pulled, she wiggled, pushing her body upward, and in a moment she was free, leaning against the tip-tilted car.

"Easy." Strong hands supported her.

"Are you sure she is all right, Calvin Burke?" This voice sounded young, a little frightened. "Should we take her to the hospital?"

"The hospital." She grasped the words. "I'm all right, but I have to get to the hospital. My sister is there. I have to go there."

She was repeating herself, she thought, her mind still a little fuzzy. She couldn't seem to help it. She focused on the three people who stood around her. An Amish couple, their young faces white and strained in the glow of the flashlight.

And the man, the one with the gruff, impatient voice and the strong, gentle hands. He held the light, so she couldn't see him well—just an impression of height, breadth, the pale cloth of his shirt.

"Your sister." His voice had sharpened. "Would you be Rachel Hampton's sister?"

"Yes." She grabbed his hand. "You know her? Do you know how she is? I keep calling, but they won't tell me anything."

"I know her. Was on my way, in fact, to see if your grandmother needed any help."

"Grams is all right, isn't she?" Her fear edged up a notch.

"Just upset over Rachel." He turned toward the young couple. "I'll take her to the hospital. You two better get along home."

"*Ja,* we will," the boy said. "We pray that your sister will be well." They both nodded and then moved quickly toward the waiting buggy, their clothing melting into the darkness.

Her Good Samaritan gestured toward the pickup truck that sat behind her car. "Anything you don't want to leave here, we can take now."

She shoved her hand through the disheveled layers of her hair, trying to think. "Overnight bag. My briefcase and computer. They're in the trunk." Concern jagged through her. "If the computer is damaged..." The project she was working on was backed up, of course, but it would still be a hassle if she couldn't work while she was here.

"I don't hear any ominous clanking noises." He pulled the cases from the trunk, whose lid gaped open. "Let's get going."

She bent over the car to retrieve her handbag and cell phone, a wave of dizziness hitting her at the movement. Gritting her teeth, she followed him to the truck.

He yanked open the passenger side door and shoved the bags onto the floor. Obviously she was meant to rest her feet on them. There was no place else to put them if she didn't want them rattling around in the back.

She climbed gingerly into the passenger seat. The dome light gave her a brief look at her rescuer as he slid behind the wheel. Thirtyish, she'd guess, with a shock of sun-streaked brown hair, longer than was fashionable, and a lean face. His shoulders were broad under the faded plaid shirt he wore, and when he gave her an impatient glance, she had the sense that he carried a chip on them.

He slammed the door, the dome light going out, and once again he was little more than an angular shape.

"I take it you know my grandmother." Small surprise, that. Katherine Unger's roots went deep in Lancaster County, back to the German immigrants who'd swarmed to Penn's Woods in the 1700s.

He nodded, and then seemed to feel something more was called for. "Cal Burke. And you're Rachel's older sister, Andrea. I've heard about you." His clipped tone suggested he hadn't been particularly impressed by whatever that was.

Still, she couldn't imagine that her sister had said anything bad about her. She and Rachel had always been close, even if they hadn't seen each other often enough in the past few years, especially since their mother's death. Even if she completely disapproved of this latest scheme Rachel and Grams had hatched.

She glanced at him. As her eyes adjusted to the dim light, she was able to see a little more, noticing his worn jeans, scuffed leather boots and a stubble of beard. She'd thought, in that first hazy glimpse as he pulled her out of the car, that he might be Amish—something about the hair, the pale shirt and dark pants. But obviously he wasn't.

"I should try the hospital again." She flipped the cell phone open.

Please. The unaccustomed prayer formed in her mind again. *Please let Rachel be all right.*

"I doubt they'll tell you any more than they already have." He frowned at the road ahead. "Have you tried your grandmother's number?"

"She never remembers to turn her cell phone on." She punched in the number anyway, only to be sent straight to voice mail. "Grams, if you get this before I see you, call me on my cell." Her throat tightened. "I hope Rachel is all right."

"Ironic," he said as she clicked off. "You have an

accident while rushing to your sister's bedside. Ever occur to you that these roads aren't meant for racing?"

She stiffened at the criticism. "I was not racing. And if you were behind me, you must have seen me brake as I approached the curve. If I hadn't..." She stopped, not wanting to imagine that.

His hands moved restlessly on the wheel, as if he wanted to push the rattletrap truck along faster but knew he couldn't. "We're coming up on Route 30. We'll make better time there."

He didn't sound conciliatory, but at least he hadn't pushed his criticism of her driving. Somehow she still wanted to defend herself.

"I'm well aware that I have to watch for buggies on this road. I just didn't expect to see anyone out this late."

And she was distracted with fear for Rachel, but she wouldn't say that to him. It would sound like a plea for sympathy.

"It's spring," he said, as if that was an explanation. "*Rumspringa,* to those kids. That means—"

"I know what *rumspringa* means," she snapped. "The time when Amish teenagers get to experience freedom and figure out what kind of life they want. You don't need to give me the Pennsylvania Dutch tour. I lived in my grandparents' house until I was ten."

"Well, I guess that makes you an expert, then."

No doubt about it, the man was annoying, but she hadn't exactly been all sweetness and light in the past half hour, either. And he was taking her to the hospital.

"Sorry. I didn't mean to snap. I guess I'm a little shaken."

He glanced at her. "Maybe you should have them check you out at the hospital. You had a rough landing."

She shook her head. "I'll probably be black-and-blue tomorrow, but that's it." She touched her neck gingerly. Either the air bag or the seat belt had left what felt like brush burns there. The bruises on her confidence from the fear she'd felt wouldn't show, but they might take longer to go away.

Apparently taking her word for it, he merged onto Route 30. The lights and activity were reassuring, and in a few minutes they pulled up at the emergency entrance to the hospital.

"Thank you." She slid out, reaching for her things. "I really appreciate this."

He spoke when she would have pulled her bag out. "I'm going in, too. May as well leave your things here until you know what you're doing."

She hesitated, and then she shrugged and let go of the case. "Fine. Thank you," she added.

He came around the truck and set off toward the entrance, his long strides making her hurry to keep up. Inside, the bright lights had her blinking. Burke caught her arm and navigated her past the check-in desk and on into the emergency room, not stopping until he reached the nurses' station.

"Evening, Ruth. This is Rachel Hampton's sister. Tell her how Rachel is without the hospital jargon, all right?"

She half expected the woman—middle-aged, gray-haired and looking as if her feet hurt—to call security. Instead she gave him a slightly flirtatious smile.

"Calvin Burke, just because you've been in here

three or four times to get stitched up, don't think you own the place." She consulted a clipboard, lips pursing.

Andrea stole a look at him. It wasn't her taste, but she supposed some women went for the rugged, disreputable-looking type.

Ruth Schmidt, according to her name badge— another good old Pennsylvania Dutch name, like Unger—picked up the telephone and had a cryptic, low-voiced conversation with someone. She hung up and gave Andrea a professional smile.

"Your sister has come through surgery fine, and she's been taken to a private room."

"What were her injuries?" She hated digging for information, as if her sister's condition were a matter of national security. "Where is my grandmother? Isn't she here?"

The woman stiffened. "I really don't know anything further about the patient's condition. I understand Mrs. Unger was persuaded to go home, as there was nothing she could do here. I'd suggest you do the same, and—"

"No." She cut the woman off. "I'm not going anywhere until I've seen my sister. And if you don't know anything about her injuries, I'll talk to someone who does."

She prepared for an argument. It didn't matter what they said to her, she wasn't leaving until she'd seen Rachel, if she had to stay here all night.

Maybe the woman recognized that. She pointed to a bank of elevators. "Third floor. Room 301. But she'll be asleep—"

She didn't wait to hear any more. She made it to the

elevator in seconds and pressed the button, the fear that had driven her since she left Philadelphia a sharp blade against her heart. Rachel would be all right. Grams wouldn't have gone home unless she was convinced of that. Still, she had to see for herself.

A quick ride in the elevator, a short walk across the hall, and she was in the room. Rachel lay motionless in the high, white hospital bed. Both legs were in casts, and hospital paraphernalia surrounded her.

Light brown hair spread out over a white pillow, dark lashes forming crescents against her cheek. Rachel looked about sixteen, instead of nearly thirty. Her little sister, whom she loved, fought with, bossed, protected. Her throat choked, and the tears she'd been holding back spilled over.

Cal picked up a five-month-old newsmagazine and slumped into a molded plastic chair. The dragons guarding the third floor wouldn't have let him in, obviously, so he'd just wait until the sister came back down again. Maybe tonight wasn't the time, but he had a few things he'd like to say to Andrea.

He frowned, uninterested, at the magazine, seeing instead the face of the woman who'd just gone upstairs. On the surface, she'd been much like he'd expected from the things her sister and grandmother had said and from the photo on Katherine's mantel.

Glossy, urban, well dressed in a rising young executive way, with silky blond hair falling to her collarbones in one of those sleek, tapered cuts that every television newswoman wore now. Eyes like green glass, sharp enough to cut a man if he weren't careful.

Well, he was a very careful man, and he knew enough not to be impressed by Ms. Andrea Hampton.

Not that her sister or grandmother had ever bad-mouthed her, but the picture had formed clearly enough in his mind from the things they said, and from her absence. Her elderly grandmother and her sister were struggling to get their bed-and-breakfast off the ground, and Ms. Successful Young Executive couldn't be bothered to leave her high-powered life long enough to help them.

Not his business, he supposed, but despite his intent to live in isolation, he'd grown fond of Katherine and her granddaughter in the time he'd been renting the barn on the Unger estate. He'd thought, when his wanderings brought him to Lancaster County, that he just wanted to be alone with his anger and his guilt. But Katherine, with her understated kindness, and Rachel, with her sweet nature, had worked their way into his heart. He felt a responsibility toward them, combined with irritation that the oldest granddaughter wasn't doing more to help.

Still, he'd been unjust to accuse her of careless driving. She'd been going the speed limit, no more, and he had seen the flash of her brake lights just before she'd rounded the curve.

Her taillights had disappeared from view, and then he'd heard the shriek of brakes, the crunch of metal, and his heart had nearly stopped. He'd rounded the curve, fearing he'd see a buggy smashed into smithereens, its passengers tossed onto the road like rag dolls.

Thank the good Lord it hadn't come to that. It had been the car, half on its side in the ditch, which had been the casualty.

Come to think of it, somebody might want to have a talk with young Jonah's father. The boy had said he'd just pulled out onto the main road from the Mueller farm. He had to have done that without paying much attention—the approaching glow of the car's lights should have been visible if he'd looked. All his attention had probably been on the pretty girl next to him.

He didn't think he'd mention that to Andrea Hampton. She might get the bright idea of suing. But he'd drop a word in Abram Yoder's ear. Not wanting to get the boy into trouble—just wanting to keep him alive.

Giving up the magazine as a lost cause, he tossed it aside and stared into space until he saw the elevator doors swish open again. Andrea came through, shoulders sagging a bit. She straightened when she saw him.

"You didn't need to wait for me."

He rose, going to her. "Yes, I did. I have your things in my truck, remember?"

Her face was pale in the fluorescent lights, mouth drooping, and those green eyes looked pink around the edges. He touched her arm.

"You want me to get you some coffee?"

She shook her head, and he had the feeling she didn't focus on his face when she looked at him. His nerves tightened.

"What is it? Rachel's going to be all right, isn't she?"

"They say so." Her voice was almost a whisper, and

then she shook her head, clearing her throat. "I'm sure they're right, but it was a shock to see her that way. Both of her legs are broken." A shiver went through her, generating a wave of sympathy that startled him. "And she has a concussion. The doctor I spoke with wouldn't even guess how long it would be until she's back to normal."

"I'm sorry to hear that." His voice roughened. Rachel didn't deserve this. No one did. He could only hope they caught the poor excuse for a human being who'd left her lying by the side of the road. If he were still an attorney, he'd take pleasure in prosecuting a case like that.

Andrea walked steadily toward the exit. Outside, she took a deep breath, pulling the tailored jacket close around her as if for warmth, even though the May night didn't have much of a bite to it.

"I'll just get my things and then you can be on your way." She managed a polite smile in his direction.

"How do you plan to get to your grandmother's? I called to have your car towed to the Churchville Garage, but I don't imagine it'll be drivable very soon."

She shoved her hair back in what seemed to be a habitual gesture. It fell silkily into place again. "Thank you. I didn't think about the car. But I'm sure I can get a taxi."

"Not so easy at this hour. I'll drive you." He yanked the door open.

"I don't want to take you out of your way. You've done enough for me already, Mr. Burke." Her tone was cool. Dismissing.

He smiled. "Cal. And you won't be taking me out of

my way. Didn't you know? I'm your grandmother's tenant."

He rather enjoyed the surprised look on her face. Petty of him, but if she kept in better contact with her grandmother, she'd know about him. Still, he suspected that if he were as good a Christian as he hoped to be, he'd cut her a bit more slack.

"I see. Well, fine then." She climbed into the truck, the skirt she wore giving him a glimpse of slim leg.

He wasn't interested in any woman right now, least of all a woman like Andrea Hampton, but that didn't mean he was dead. He could still appreciate beautiful, and that's what Andrea was, with that pale oval face, soft mouth and strong jawline. Come to think of it, she'd gotten the stubborn chin from her grandmother, who was as feisty a seventy-some-year-old as he'd met in a long time.

She didn't speak as he drove out of the hospital lot. He didn't mind. God had been teaching him patience in the past year or so, something he'd never thought of before as a virtue. He suspected she'd find it necessary to break the silence sooner than he would.

Sure enough, they'd barely hit the highway when she stirred. "You said you were my grandmother's tenant. Does that mean you're living in the house?" Her hands moved restlessly. "Or inn, I guess I should say, given Grams and Rachel's project."

She didn't approve, then. He could hear it in her voice.

"I rent the barn from your grandmother. The newer one, behind the house. I've been there for six months now, and in the area for nearly a year."

Healing. Atoning for his mistakes and trying to get right with God, but that was something he didn't say to anyone.

"The barn?" Her voice rose in question. "What do you want with the barn? Do you mean you live there?"

He shrugged. "I fixed up the tack room for a small apartment. Comfortable enough for one. I run my business in the rest of it."

"What business?" She sounded suspicious.

He was tempted to make something up, but he guessed she'd had enough shocks tonight. "I design and make wood furniture, using Amish techniques. If you pick up any wood shavings on your clothes, that's why."

"I see." The tone reserved judgment. "Grams never mentioned it to me."

"Well, you haven't been around much, have you?"

He caught the flash of anger in her face, even keeping his eyes on the road.

"I speak with my grandmother and my sister every week, and they came to stay with me at Easter, not that it's any of your concern."

They were coming into the village now, and he slowed. There wasn't much traffic in Churchville, or even many lights on, at this hour. The antique shops and quilt stores that catered to tourists were long since closed.

He pulled into the drive of the gracious, Federal-style Unger mansion, its Pennsylvania sandstone glowing a soft gold in the light from the twin lampposts he'd erected for Katherine. He stopped at the door.

He wouldn't be seeing much of Andrea, he'd guess.

She'd scurry back to her busy career as soon as she was convinced her sister would recover, the anxiety she'd felt tonight fading under the frenzied rush of activity that passed for a life.

"Thank you." She snapped off the words as she opened the door, grabbing her bags, obviously still annoyed at his presumption.

"No problem."

She slammed the door, and he pulled away, leaving her standing under the hand-carved sign that now hung next to the entrance to the Unger mansion. The Three Sisters Inn.

TWO

Andrea had barely reached the recessed front door when it was flung open, light spilling out onto the flagstones. In an instant she was in Grams's arms, and the tears she didn't want to shed flowed. They stood half in and half out of the house, and she was ten again, weeping over the mess her parents were making of their lives, holding on to Grams and thinking that here was one rock she could always cling to.

Grams drew her inside, blotting her tears with an unsteady hand, while her own trickled down her cheeks. "I'm so glad you're here, Dree. So glad."

The childhood nickname, given when two-years-younger Rachel couldn't say her name, increased the sensation that she'd stepped into the past. She stood in the center hall that had seemed enormous to her once, with its high ceiling and wide plank floor. Barney, Grams's sheltie, danced around them, welcoming her with little yips.

She bent to pet the dog, knowing Barney wouldn't stop until she did. "I went to the hospital to see Rachel.

They told me you'd already gone home. I should have called you...."

Grams shook her head, stopping her. "It's fine. Cal phoned me while you were with Rachel."

"He didn't say." Her tone was dry. Nice of him, but he might have mentioned he'd talked to Grams.

"He told me about the accident." Grams's arm, still strong and wiry despite her age, encircled Andrea's waist. Piercing blue eyes, bone structure that kept her beautiful despite her wrinkles, a pair of dangling aqua earrings that matched the blouse she wore—Grams looked great for any age, let alone nearly seventy-five. "Two accidents in one night is two too many."

That was a typical Grams comment, the tartness of her tone hiding the fear she must have felt.

"Well, fortunately the only damage was to the car." She'd better change the subject, before Grams started to dwell on might-have-beens. She looked through the archway to the right, seeing paint cloths draped over everything in the front parlor. "I see you're in the midst of redecorating."

Grams's blue eyes darkened with worry. "The opening is Memorial Day weekend, and now Rachel is laid up. I don't know..." She stopped and shook her head. "Well, we'll get through it somehow. Right now, let's get you settled, so that both of us can catch a few hours sleep. Tomorrow will be here before you know it."

"Where are you putting me?" She glanced up the graceful open staircase that led from the main hall to the second floor. "Is that all guest rooms now?"

Grams nodded. "The west side of the house is the inn. The east side is still ours." She opened the door on the left of the hall. "Come along in. We have the back stairway and the rooms on this side, so that'll give us our privacy. You'll be surprised at how well this is working out."

She doubted it, but she was too tired to pursue the subject now. Or to think straight, for that matter. And Grams must be exhausted, physically and emotionally. Still, she couldn't help one question.

"What was she doing out there? Rachel, I mean. Why was she walking along Crossings Road alone after dark?"

"She was taking Barney for a run." Grams's voice choked a little. "She's been doing that for me since she got here, especially now that things have been so upset. Usually there's not much traffic."

That made sense. Rachel could cut onto Crossings Road, perpendicular to the main route, without going into the village.

She trailed her grandmother through the large room that had been her grandfather's library, now apparently being converted into an office-living room, and up the small, enclosed stairway. This was the oldest part of the house, built in 1725. The ceilings were lower here, accounting for lots of odd little jogs in how the two parts of the Unger mansion fit together.

Grams held on to the railing, as if she needed some help getting up the stairs, but her back was as straight as ever. The dog, who always slept on the rug beside her bed, padded along.

Her mind flickered back to Grams's comment. "What do you mean, things have been upset? Has something gone wrong with your plans?"

She could have told them, had told them, that they were getting in over their heads with this idea of turning the place into an inn. Neither of them knew anything about running a bed-and-breakfast, and Grams was too old for this kind of stress.

"Just—just the usual things. Nothing for you to worry about."

That sounded evasive. She'd push, but they were both too tired.

Her grandmother opened a door at the top of the stairs. "Here we are. I thought you'd want your old room."

The ceiling sloped, and the rosebud wallpaper hadn't changed in twenty years. Even her old rag doll, left behind when her mother had stormed out of the house with them, still sat in the rocking chair, and her white Bible lay on the bedside table. This had been her room until she was ten, until the cataclysm that split the family and sent them flying off in all directions, like water droplets from a tornado. She tossed her bags onto the white iron bed and felt like crying once more.

"Thanks, Grams." Her voice was choked.

"It's all right." Grams gave her another quick hug. "Let's just have a quick prayer." She clasped Andrea's hands, and Andrea tried not to think about how long it had been since she'd prayed before tonight.

"Hold our Rachel in Your hands, Father." Grams's voice was husky. "We know You love her even more than we do. Please, touch her with Your healing hand. Amen."

"Amen," Andrea whispered. She was sure there were questions she should ask, but her mind didn't seem to be working clearly.

"Night, Grams. Try and sleep."

"Good night, Dree. I'm so glad you're here." Grams left the door ajar, her footsteps muffled on the hall carpet as she went to the room across the hall.

Andrea looked at her things piled on the bed, and it seemed a gargantuan effort to move them. She undressed slowly, settling in.

She took her shirt off and winced at the movement, turning to the wavy old mirror to see what damage she'd done. Bruises on her chest and shoulder were dark and ugly where the seat belt had cut in, and she had brush burns from the air bag. She was lucky that was the worst of it, but she shook a little at the reminder.

After pulling a sleep shirt over her head, she cleaned off the bed and turned back the covers. She'd see about her car in the morning. Call the office, explain that she wouldn't be in for a few days. Her boss wouldn't like that, not with the Waterburn project nearing completion. Well, she couldn't make any decisions until she saw how Rachel was.

Frustration edged along her nerves as she crossed to the window to pull down the shade, not wanting to wake with the sun. This crazy scheme to turn the mansion into a bed-and-breakfast had been Rachel's idea, no doubt. She hadn't really settled to anything since culinary school, always moving from job to job.

Grams should have talked some sense into her, instead of going along with the idea. At this time in her life, Grams deserved a quiet, peaceful retirement. And Rachel should be finding a job that had some security to it.

Andrea didn't like risky gambles. Maybe that was what made her such a good financial manager. Financial security came first, and then other things could line up behind it. If she'd learned anything from those chaotic years when her mother had dragged them around the country, constantly looking for something to make her happy, it was that.

She stood for a moment, peering out. From this window she looked over the roof of the sunroom, added on to the back of the house overlooking the gardens when Grams had come to the Unger mansion as a bride. There was the pond, a little gleam of light striking the water, and the gazebo. Other shadowy shapes were various outbuildings. Behind them loomed the massive bulk of the old barn that had predated even the house. Off to the right, toward the neighboring farm, was the "new" barn, dating to the 1920s.

It was dark now, with Cal presumably asleep in the tack room apartment. Well, he was another thing to worry about tomorrow. She lowered the shade with a decisive snap and went to crawl into bed.

Her eyes closed. She was tired, so tired. She'd sleep, and deal with all of it in the morning.

Something creaked overhead—once, then again. She stiffened, imagining a stealthy footstep in the connecting attics that stretched over the wings of the house. She strained to listen, clutching the sheet against her, but the sound wasn't repeated.

Old houses make noises, she reminded herself. Particularly her grandmother's, if her childhood memories were any indicator. She was overreacting. That faint, scratching sound was probably a mouse, safely distant from her. Tired muscles relaxed into the soft bed, and exhaustion swept over her.

She plummeted into sleep, as if she dived into a deep, deep pool.

Andrea stepped out onto the patio from the breakfast room, Barney nosing out behind her and then running off toward the pond, intent on his own pursuits. A positive call from the hospital had lifted a weight from her shoulders and she felt able to deal with other things. She paused to look around and take a deep breath of country air.

Not such pleasant country air, she quickly discovered. Eli Zook must be spreading manure on his acreage, which met the Unger property on two sides. How were the city tourists Rachel expected to have as guests going to like that? Maybe they'd be pleased at the smell of a genuine Amish farm.

They'd have to admire the view from the breakfast room. The flagstone patio had stood the years well, and now it was brightened by pots overflowing with pansies and ageratum. The wide flower bed dazzled with peonies and daylilies. She had knelt there next to Grams, learning to tell a weed from a flower.

Moving a little stiffly, thanks to her bruises, she

stepped over the low patio wall and followed the flagstone path that led back through the farther reaches of the garden, weaving around the pond and past the gazebo with its white Victorian gingerbread. When she glanced back at the house, morning sunlight turned the sandstone to mellow gold, making the whole building glow.

Rounding the small potting shed, she came face-to-face with the new barn. An apt expression, because she'd always thought the barn had more character than a lot of people. Lofty, white, a traditional bank barn with entries on two levels, it had the stone foundation and hip roof that characterized Pennsylvania Dutch barns. More properly Pennsylvania Swiss or German, her grandfather had always said, but the name stuck.

It hadn't seen much use since her grandfather had stopped farming and leased the fields to the Zook family, but the stone foundation showed no sign of deterioration, and the wooden planks looked as if they had a fresh coat of white paint.

A small sign on the upper level door was the only indication that Cal Burke did business here. And how much business could he do, really? The only way into his shop was via the rutted lane that ran along a hedge of overgrown lilacs that bordered the house. She glanced toward the road. Yes, there was a tiny sign there, too, one that could hardly be read from a passing car. The man needed a few lessons in marketing.

She walked up the bank to the door and tapped lightly. Stepping inside, she inhaled the scent of wood shavings and hay. Music poured from a CD player that sat on a wooden bench. Cal apparently liked Mozart to work by. He bent over a pie safe, totally absorbed as he fitted a pierced tin insert to a door.

He obviously hadn't heard her, so she glanced around, wanting to see any changes before she spoke to him. There weren't many. In the center threshing floor he'd installed a workbench and tools, and the rest of the space was taken up with pieces of furniture in various stages of construction. The mows and lofts on either side already held hay and straw, probably stored there by Eli Zook.

She took a step forward, impressed in spite of herself by his work. They were simple oak pieces, for the most part, done in the classic style of Pennsylvania Dutch furniture. There was a three-drawer chest with graceful carving incised on the drawer fronts, a chest stenciled with typical tulips and hearts, a rocking chair with a curved back.

Cal did have a gift for this work, and he was certainly focused. Sun-bleached hair swung forward in his eyes, and he pushed it back with a sweep of one hand, all of his movements smooth and unhurried. He wore faded jeans and a blue plaid shirt, also faded, the sleeves rolled up to the elbows. A shaft of sunlight, beaming down from the open loft door, seemed to put him in a spotlight, picking out gold in his brown hair and glinting off tanned forearms.

She moved slightly just as the music stopped. The sole of her loafer rustled stray wood shavings, and he looked up. The pierced tin clattered to the floor, the sound loud in the sudden stillness.

"I'm sorry. I didn't mean to disturb you."

"It's all right." He straightened, leaning against the pie safe, and watched her approach.

She hadn't noticed his eyes last night. The light had been too dim, for the most part, and she'd been too upset. Now she saw that they were a light, warm brown, flecked with gold like his hair.

He waited until she stopped, a few feet from him, before he spoke again. "Any news from the hospital?"

"We called first thing. Rachel had a good night, and she's awake and asking for us." She couldn't stop the smile that blossomed on the words.

"Thank God." He smiled in return, strong lips curving, lines crinkling around his eyes, his whole face lighting. For an instant she couldn't look away, and something seemed to shimmer between them, as light and insubstantial as the dust motes in the shaft of sunshine.

She turned to look at the furniture, feeling a need to evade his glance for a moment. She wouldn't want him to think he had any effect on her.

"So this is your work." She touched a drop leaf table. "Cherry, isn't it?"

He nodded, moving next to her and stroking the wood as if it were a living thing. "I've been working mostly in oak and pine, but Emma Zook wanted a cherry table, and Eli had some good lengths of cherry that I could use."

"It's beautiful. Emma will be delighted, although if I remember Amish customs correctly, she won't say so."

A faint smile flickered in his eyes. "'For use, not for

pretty,' she'll say. Anything else might sound like pride."

"That's Emma, all right." Nostalgia swept through her. Emma Zook had helped Grams in the house for years, and her sturdy figure, always clad in a long dress and apron, was present in Andrea's earliest memories.

As children, they'd played with the Zook youngsters, so used to them that they never saw the Amish clothing or dialect as odd. She'd caught up a bit with Emma over breakfast. As she'd expected, all the children except Levi were married and parents by now. Levi—well, Levi would always be a child, no matter how old he was.

"The Amish have the right idea," Cal said. "No reason why something can't be both useful and beautiful."

She traced the scalloped edge of the drop leaf. "This certainly qualifies."

"Two compliments in as many minutes." He drew back in mock surprise.

"I believe in giving credit where credit is due. You make lovely furniture. I just can't help but wonder why you're doing it in my grandmother's barn."

Where did you come from, and why are you here? That's what she was really asking. How could this man have made such inroads into her family when she hadn't even known about him?

He shrugged. "I came to this area to learn Amish furniture techniques. When I needed a place to set up shop, she had an empty barn. We came to an agreement."

She'd like to ask what that agreement was, but he

could answer that it wasn't her business. Which it wasn't, but anything that affected her grandmother and sister mattered to her, whether she'd been back recently or not.

"You're not from around here," she tried.

"No. I'm not."

Most people liked talking about themselves. Cal Burke seemed to be the exception.

"You're a little hard to find. How do you market your work?"

He shrugged again. "There are plenty of machine-made copies out there, but if people are asking around for good, handmade furniture done in the old Amish style, they'll find me or one of the others who do it."

"That's no way to do business." His marketing strategy, if that's what it was, exasperated her so much that she couldn't stop the words. "You have something people want, so make it easy to find you. You could probably double or triple your business if you did a little advertising."

"I don't want to double my business. There are only so many pieces I can make by hand in a month, and they sell okay. What am I going to do with more customers than I can satisfy?"

She blinked, looking at him. As far as she could tell, he was serious. "If you hired a few people to help you—"

"Then it wouldn't be my furniture people were buying."

"But you could make more money—"

He shook his head with an impatient movement that made the hair flop in his eyes again. "I make enough to get by, and I enjoy my work. Your corporate approach wouldn't work for me."

She stiffened. "If you mean I'm practical, I don't consider that an insult. Although I suspect you meant it that way."

"Just recognizing a difference in how we see things, that's all." His voice was mild, but his eyes had turned frosty. "If you came out here to tell me how to run my business, I thank you for your interest."

"No." She bit off the word. The world needed practical people like her. They kept the dreamers afloat. But she didn't suppose it would do any good to tell him so. "My grandmother wants you to know that we'll be going to the hospital shortly. She asks if you'll keep an eye out for the painters and let them in." Somehow it seemed important that he know the favor was for Grams, not her.

"I'd be glad to."

"I thought she could call you, but she said you never answer your phone."

"Really bugs you, doesn't it?" His expression suggested internal laughter. "I don't like to jump when the phone rings. If anybody wants me, they leave a message."

She bit back another comment about his business methods. Or lack of them. Why should she care if the man frittered away his prospects for want of a few sensible steps?

"I see." She kept her tone perfectly polite. "Thank you for taking care of the painters. My grandmother will appreciate it."

She turned and walked away quickly, suspecting that if she looked back, she'd find an amused smile on his face.

"But I can't. I really can't." Andrea looked from her grandmother to her sister. Both faces were turned toward hers, both expectant, waiting for an answer she couldn't possibly give. "I'm extremely busy at work right now."

"Surely your employer will give you the time off." Grams was serenely confident. "Your family needs you."

Rachel didn't say anything. She just leaned back against the raised head of the hospital bed, her face almost as white as the pillow.

She'd tell herself they were ganging up on her, but that wasn't true. They were depending on her, just as Rachel and baby sister Caroline had depended on her during those years when Mom had relocated the family from place to place, nursing her grudge against Grams and Grandfather and depriving her children of the only stable home they'd ever known.

Andrea was the oldest. She was the responsible one. She'd take care of it.

The trouble was, she was responsible to her job, as well, and there couldn't possibly be a worse time for her to take off. Gordon Walker would not understand his right-hand woman requesting a leave to help her family. He hadn't even taken time away from work when his wife was in labor with their twins.

Of course, he and his wife were now divorced, and he saw his daughters once a month if he was lucky.

She tried again. "I'm in the middle of a very important project, and I'm on a deadline. I couldn't take time off now. It wouldn't be fair to the company."

It wasn't fair to her, either. Maybe that thought was unworthy, but she couldn't help it. The promotion her boss had been dangling in front of her for the past year would be hers when this project was completed. Her position with the company, her stable, secure life, would be assured.

"Can't someone else take over for you?" Grams's brow furrowed. "We've already accepted reservations for our opening weekend. All the rooms are booked. We can't turn those people away now."

Grams's sense of hospitality was obviously offended at the thought, even though these would be paying guests. Andrea could see it in her eyes. An Unger didn't let people down.

I'm a Hampton, too. She thought bleakly of her father. They're pretty good at letting people down.

Rachel tried to push herself up on the bed a little, wincing, and Andrea hurried to help her.

"Take it easy. I don't think you should try to do that on your own. Those casts must weigh a ton."

"If they don't, they feel like it." Rachel moved her head restlessly on the pillow.

Looking into Rachel's eyes was like looking in a mirror. Green eyes, cat's eyes. All three Hampton girls had them, even though otherwise they didn't look at all alike.

She was the cool, conservative blonde. That was how people saw her, and she didn't find anything wrong with that. It fit with who she wanted to be.

Rachel, two years younger, was the warm one, with her heart-shaped face and her sunny-brown hair. She had the gift of making friends and collecting strays everywhere she went. Sweet, generous, she was the family peacemaker, always the buffer.

And they'd needed a buffer, she and Caroline. Her youngest sister had been born an exotic orchid in a family of daisies. She certainly looked the part. In her, the green eyes sparkled and shot fire. Her hair, a rich, deep red, had been worn in a mass of curls to below her shoulders the last time Andrea had seen her. Currently, as far as she knew, Caroline was making pottery in Taos. Or maybe it was turquoise jewelry in Santa Fe. Andrea couldn't keep up.

"I could come home in a wheelchair. We could get some extra help and I could supervise." But the tears that shone in Rachel's eyes belied the brave words, and she thumped one hand against the side rail of the bed, making the IV clatter.

"Honey, don't." Andrea caught the restless hand, her heart twisting. "It'll be all right."

But how would it be all right? How could she be true to herself and yet not let them down?

Rachel clung to her, much as she had when Mom had taken them away from Grams and Grandfather so many years ago. "You mean you'll do it?"

"We'll find some way of handling the situation. I promise."

Rachel gave a little sigh, relaxing a bit, though worry still puckered her brows.

"Good," Grams said. "I knew we could count on you."

She'd told her boss she couldn't be back until Monday, though she'd continue working while she was here. She was only a phone call or an e-mail away, after all. By then, she'd somehow convince Grams and Rachel that with Rachel laid up for who knows how long, starting a bed-and-breakfast didn't make sense.

A glance at Rachel's face assured her that now was not the time to mention that. Rachel was far too fragile.

She'd discuss it with Grams later. Giving up the inn was the best thing for everyone, especially Rachel. Once she was healed, she could get another restaurant job in a minute with her skills, and if she needed help to get through until then, Andrea or Grams would certainly provide that.

Right now she had to do something to wipe that strained expression from Rachel's eyes. "Did you hear about my adventure getting here last night? Rescued from a ditch by your handsome tenant. Hope you don't mind my using your car while mine's in the body shop."

"Grams told me Cal brought you to the hospital. He is a hunk, isn't he?" Some of the tension eased out of the pale face. "So, you interested, big sis?"

"I wouldn't want to tread on your territory." She smiled. "We made a deal a long time ago, remember? No boyfriend poaching."

"Sad to say, Cal doesn't see me as anything but little-sister material." She wrinkled her nose. "I have to admit, when I first met him, I thought there might be something, but the chemistry just isn't there."

Andrea didn't bother to analyze why she was

relieved. "I understand he's been around for about a year?" She made it a question for both of them.

"Just about," Grams agreed. "He stayed over at the Zimmerman farm for a while, I think, when he first came to the area."

"You never mentioned renting the barn to him when we talked." Grams and Rachel had come into the city for dinner just a month ago, but in all their talk about the inn, they hadn't brought up their resident tenant.

"Didn't we? I thought you knew about him."

The vagueness of it got under her skin. "Where did he come from? What did he do before? What does Uncle Nick think of him?" Her grandfather's business partner had a solid, no-nonsense attitude that Grams lacked.

"I don't know. Does it matter?" Grams frowned a little, as if Andrea had said something impolite. "And it's not James Bendick's business."

Rachel moved slightly. "He's a nice guy. That's all we need to know."

It wasn't all *she* needed to know. Perhaps the truth was that Grams hadn't mentioned him because she'd known exactly the questions Andrea would ask and didn't want to answer them. Grams did things her own way, and she'd never appreciated unsolicited advice.

"I believe I'll get some coffee." Grams stood, picking up her handbag.

"I'll get it for you, Grams," she offered.

Her grandmother shook her head. "You stay here and talk to Rachel. I want to stretch my legs a bit."

Andrea watched her leave, her heart clutching a little.

Grams wouldn't admit it, but she was slowing down. Grams had always been so strong, so unchanging, that age had sat lightly upon her. It had seemed she would never let it get the better of her. But that had been an illusion.

A weight settled on Andrea's shoulders. She had to make the right decisions now. Rachel, Grams—she was responsible for both of them.

"Are you okay, Dree?"

She shook off the apprehension before she turned to look at her sister. "Sure. Just worried about you. Did the police talk to you about the accident?"

Rachel nodded. "The township chief was in before you got here. It doesn't sound as if they have much evidence. He wanted to know if I remembered anything."

"Do you?"

Rachel moved restlessly. "I don't remember anything that happened after about noon yesterday."

THREE

Cal let himself in the side door of the Unger mansion, toolbox in hand. He'd told Katherine that he'd fix the loose post on the main staircase, but that wasn't his only reason for being there.

He'd been mulling it over, praying about it, most of the day. Prayer was still new enough to him that he wondered sometimes whether he ought to be asking for guidance about simple everyday things. Still, it was comforting to feel that Someone cared.

And this wasn't a selfish thing. He wanted a sense of whether he should speak to Andrea about her grandmother. Seemed to him the answer was yes, although that might just be his need to do something.

Two years ago, he'd have found it laughable to think he'd be so concerned about an elderly woman who wasn't even a relative, but he hadn't been much of a human being, either, back then. Now—well, he cared about Katherine Unger.

Katherine was kind, proud and too stubborn to ask for help even when she needed it. She'd be appalled, probably, if she realized how much he'd learned about her concerns just by listening. If she knew he intended to talk to Andrea, she'd be outraged.

But someone had to. Emma Zook could, but she might be too much in awe of Katherine to do it. So he would. He reached the stairs and pulled out a hammer. He'd been watching for an opportunity to speak to Andrea alone since she'd returned from the hospital, but she'd been holed up in the second-floor family quarters. Maybe a little noise would draw her out.

Sure enough, it didn't take more than a few hearty blows with the hammer before Andrea appeared at the top of the stairs, looking annoyed. She marched down to him.

"What are you doing?" She'd exchanged the pants and jacket she'd been wearing this morning for a pair of dark jeans and a green top that matched her eyes. "I'm trying to do some work upstairs."

"Sorry. You brought work with you?"

"Of course. I couldn't just walk out in the middle of the week."

Even when rushing to her sister's side, she hadn't left the job that seemed so important to her. She reminded him of himself, the way he used to be. That probably went a long way toward explaining why she annoyed him so much. He wasn't too fond of that guy.

He rested his elbow on the banister. "Wouldn't your boss give you a break under the circumstances?"

For a moment she hesitated, and he could almost read her thoughts. She had the kind of superior who wouldn't, as a matter of fact, and she didn't want to admit it.

"I didn't ask," she said finally. "I have responsibilities, and I meet them." She frowned. "What are you doing here, anyway?"

"Katherine asked me to take care of this loose place in the banister." He wiggled the carved wood gently, mindful of its delicate reeding. "I had time to get to it this afternoon."

"I didn't realize you work for my grandmother."

"I don't. I'm just being neighborly." He still hadn't figured out the best approach. "Look, I know this is none of my business—"

"But it's not going to stop you," she finished for him. "All right. You won't be content until you have your say, so get it over with." She planted one hand on the railing, standing up a step so that their faces were level.

"You don't beat around the bush, do you?"

"I try not to." A slight frown appeared between her brows. "Does that bother you?"

"On the contrary, it makes it easier." If she wanted it straight from the hip, she'd get it. "Your grandmother and sister have been running themselves ragged, trying to get the inn ready. They needed help even before Rachel was hurt, but now it's worse. With Rachel in the hospital, your grandmother shouldn't be in the house alone. Did she tell you she's spotted a prowler out in the grounds recently?"

She sent him a startled glance, hand tightening on the railing. "No. Did she call the police?"

"By the time they got here, the person was long gone." He shrugged. "They didn't take it too seriously, figuring it was just someone curious about the inn. Still, there have been some minor incidents of vandalism in the area lately and a few break-ins. I've been trying to keep an eye on things. But she shouldn't be staying here at night by herself."

"You're right about that." She sounded faintly bewildered that she was agreeing with him. "As for the rest, I'm not sure how best to help her."

He was surprised that she was taking it so well, but perhaps she'd been giving some thought to the problem. She just hadn't come to the right conclusion yet.

"Move in, take over for Rachel, get the inn up and running," he said promptly. "Your grandmother can't do it by herself."

"My job—"

"—can get along without you for a while."

"You don't know that." If her glare had been a blow, it would have knocked him over. "I'd be risking a lot to stay here now."

"I get it. I had bosses like that once." He had a feeling he'd *been* that kind of a boss.

"Then you should understand. Maybe I can hire someone to help out."

He shook his head. "I'm not saying more workers wouldn't make things go faster, but what's needed is someone to oversee the whole project. Your grandmother isn't up to that anymore."

"You think I don't know that?" She fired up instantly. "She shouldn't be attempting something so ambitious at her age. She ought to just relax and enjoy life."

"How is she supposed to do that? What's she going

to live on, air?" He clamped his mouth shut. He'd gone too far, even though his intentions were good.

"What are you implying?" She grabbed his arm to keep him from stepping away. "My grandmother doesn't need to worry about money."

Was she putting on a front?

"Maybe you ought to have a serious conversation with your grandmother."

Her grip tightened. "Tell me what you meant. What do you know, or think you know?"

Fine, then. "I know I offered to lend her the money for the renovations, but she took out a loan on the house instead. I know Emma works for free half the time. I know the signs of financial trouble. If someone doesn't step in, namely you, your grandmother could lose this place that means the world to her."

He yanked his arm free and grabbed the toolbox.

"I'll come back later and fix this."

Andrea was actually shaking. She watched Cal's broad back as he retreated down the hall. She should talk to Grams—no, she should find out first from someone she trusted if there was any truth to Cal's allegations. Emma. Emma knew everything that went on here.

But even as she thought it, there was a tap on the front door, followed by a quick, "Anyone here?"

"Uncle Nick." She hurried to the door, to be swept into a hug. Soft whiskers and a scent of peppermint— that was Uncle Nick.

He held her at arm's length. "Well, if you're not a sight

for sore eyes, Andrea. You're looking beautiful, as always."

"And you're the biggest flatterer in town, as always. You haven't aged a bit."

She made the expected response automatically, but it was true. Maybe the beard and hair were a little whiter, his figure in the neat blue suit just a bit stouter, but his cheeks were still rosy and firm as apples. He had an aura of permanence and stability that was very welcome.

"Ah, don't tell me that. I know better." He shook his head. "This is a sad business about Rachel."

She linked her arm with his. "She's going to make a complete recovery—the doctors have promised. Come into the library. We have to talk."

He lifted bushy white eyebrows. "Where's your grandmother?"

"Taking a nap, thank goodness. She needs one, after yesterday's upsets."

He nodded, glancing around the room and taking in the computer setup and file cabinets. "It's sad to see this fine old room turned into an office. What your grandfather would have said, I don't know."

There didn't seem to be an answer to that. She gestured him to a chair, sitting down opposite him.

He was surveying her with shrewd, kind blue eyes. "You're worried, aren't you? Tell Uncle Nick about it."

She had to smile. He wasn't really their uncle, nor was his name Nick. Caroline had called him that when she was three because to her eyes, James Bendick, Grandfather's junior partner, looked like St. Nicholas.

"That's what you always said. And you solved our problems with chocolate and peppermints."

"It's a good solution."

"Not for this problem." The worry, dissipated for a moment in the pleasure of seeing him, weighed on her again. "Tell me the truth, Uncle Nick. Is Grams in financial trouble?"

"Who told you that? Not your grandmother." His voice had sharpened.

"No. Cal Burke told me. He seems to think she could lose the house."

"I'd call that an exaggeration." He frowned. "And I'm not sure what business it is of his, in any event."

"Never mind him. Tell me what's going on. I thought Grandfather left her well-off. I've never questioned that."

"Your grandmother never questioned it, either. Sad to say, maybe she should have."

"But the properties, his investments…" She couldn't believe it. "Explain it to me."

Uncle Nick's lips puckered. "I'm not sure I should. Your grandmother—"

"Grams is depending on me." Normally she'd appreciate his discretion, but not now. "I have to know what's wrong in order to help her."

He hesitated, looking distressed. Finally he nodded. "Your grandfather decided, a few years before his death, to sell most of his properties. He didn't want to take care of them."

"I thought he enjoyed that." One of her earliest memories was of riding along with Grandpa when he went out the first day of every month to collect the rents from his tenants. That had been her first taste of business, and she'd wanted to be just like him.

Uncle Nick shrugged. "People change. He wanted to invest the money himself." His gaze dropped. "He wasn't very good. If only he'd held on to the property until the real estate market went up, your grandmother would be sitting pretty."

"As it is…" She could hardly take it in. Still, she'd certainly known how determined Grandpa was to do as he chose. Something chilled inside her. She, of all people, knew just how stubborn he could be.

"She has this place left, but not enough to maintain it." His voice was brisk, as if he didn't want to dwell on what had been. "I'm not sure how you feel about this idea of theirs to turn the place into an inn."

"I think it's a bad move," she said promptly. "Rachel is a great cook, but she doesn't know anything about running an inn. And Grams doesn't need the stress at her age."

Nick beamed at her as if they were the only two sensible people left on earth. "The practical course is for your grandmother to sell. She could pay off the home equity loan she took for the renovations and have enough to live very comfortably for the rest of her life."

"I wish she agreed."

He nodded. "She has her own stubborn streak, that's for sure. I was worried about her living here alone since your grandfather died, but she'd never listen to me. It was a little better after Rachel moved back, but even so…"

"Cal Burke is out at the barn." With the phone he never answered. What good did that do?

"Burke." He repeated the name. "I suppose he's better than nothing, but what do we know about him?"

Not much. She shared his concern.

"And there have been a rash of thefts. People breaking into isolated farmhouses. You know what this area is like—folks have lived here for generations, never giving a thought that Great-aunt Eva's dough box might be worth a small fortune to a crooked dealer."

She almost wished she hadn't asked, but it was better to face the facts, no matter how unpleasant.

"What are we going to do?" It was good to feel that she had an ally. "Rachel and Grams want me to stay and open the inn. They don't seem to understand that I have a position I can't walk away from."

He patted her hand. "If you make it clear you can't, they'd have to face facts."

"I've tried. Without success."

"You'll have to keep trying." He rose. "Give my best to your grandmother, and tell Rachel that I'll see her later." He gave her a quick hug. "I know you'll do the right thing. You always do."

"Can I carry that for you, Andrea?"

Andrea stopped reluctantly. She'd noticed Cal down the block when she'd left Snyder's General Store to walk back to the house, but she hadn't been eager to talk to him. Just because he was right about her grandmother's finances didn't mean she had to like it.

He caught up with her, and she handed over the shopping bag, taking in the dress shirt and neat gray slacks he wore. She blinked, exaggerating her surprise.

"You didn't know I'd clean up this well, did you?" He smiled, apparently ready to forgive and forget.

"Have a hot date?"

"No, just out for supper at the Dutch Inn. It's chicken and dumpling night. What about you?"

She gestured toward the bag he now carried. "Grams needed a few things from the store, and I didn't want to drive to New Holland to the supermarket."

"So you went to Snyder's, where you get a hot serving of gossip with every bag of groceries."

She couldn't stop a smile. "Some things never change."

"Did you get the latest popular opinion on who I am and why I'm here?"

She was surprised that he spoke so easily about it. "Opinion is divided. You're either a famous author hiding from a deranged fan or a bank robber sitting on his loot until it cools off. That one came from Etta Snyder's ten-year-old son. Her teenage daughter considers you a tragic figure recovering from a terrible loss."

She felt a sudden qualm. What if any of them proved true?

But he didn't seem affected. "I'll let you guess which it is." They walked past the Village Soda Shop and Longstreet's Antiques, their steps matching. "Did you get the whole scoop from Bendick? I saw him come in."

She stiffened. Her family troubles weren't his affair. Didn't he understand that?

His eyebrows lifted. "Okay. Right. I'm interfering."

She fought with herself for a moment. Interfering.

Aggravating. But he already knew, so who was she kidding by refusing to answer him?

"Uncle Nick confirmed what you said." She bit off the words, resenting the fact that he'd known what she should have.

"Sorry. I wish I'd been wrong." His voice had just the right degree of sympathy.

Some of her resentment ebbed away. This wasn't his fault. "I can't grasp it. When I was small, I thought my grandfather was the wisest, kindest man in the world."

Her opinion about the kindness had changed when Grandfather let them go without a word, writing them out of his life except for the college funds he'd provided. Surely he could have mended the quarrel with Mom if he'd really cared about them. But even so, she'd never doubted his business acumen.

"You can still have good memories of him." His tone warmed.

She could only nod, her throat choking up. She would like to remember Grandfather as she'd once seen him, without thinking about how he'd let her and her sisters down. Or how he'd apparently failed Grams.

"Why didn't my grandmother tell me? I would have helped."

She could feel his gaze on her face. "Maybe it doesn't matter why. Now that you know, you'll do the right thing."

He sounded like an echo of Uncle Nick, except that they didn't agree about what that right thing was.

"Uncle Nick told me he's been worried about Grams. He said there have been problems with antique thieves.

That prowler you mentioned—" She came to a stop, frowning at him.

He stopped, too, leaning an elbow on top of the stone wall that surrounded the church across the street from Grams's house. "Could be connected, I suppose."

"Nick said they hit isolated farmhouses. Grams's place is right on the edge of the village."

"It's also big, concealed by plenty of trees and outbuildings, and for the most part has had only one elderly woman in residence. There aren't any houses to the east, and in the back, the farms are too far away for troublemakers to be spotted." His frown deepened as he looked across the road toward the house.

She shivered a little at the thought. He was right— the mansion was isolated in spite of the fact that it fronted on the main road. Crossings Road, where Rachel had been injured, snaked along one side, leading toward distant farms and making it easy for someone to approach from the back. "Surely no one would try to break into the house."

"They wouldn't have to. The outbuildings are crammed to the roof with stuff. Furniture, mostly. And that's not including the attics of the house itself. No one knows what's there."

"You mean there's no inventory?"

His lips twisted in a wry smile. "I'm sure you'd have a tidy inventory, with the approximate value listed for every item."

"Of course I would." Her voice was tart. He didn't need to act as if efficiency were a sin. "For insurance purposes, if nothing else."

"That's how your mind works, but not your grandmother's."

"I suppose not." Her grandmother was an odd mixture—clever about people, but naive about business, which had been her husband's prerogative. "You're trying to give me nightmares, aren't you?"

He gave a rueful smile and shoved away from the wall. "Sorry about that." He touched her hand in a brief gesture of sympathy. Warmth shimmered across her skin and was gone. "I figured I shouldn't be the only one."

Andrea was still wrestling with the difficulties when she went up to her room that evening, hoping to concentrate on some work. A half-dozen times she'd nearly confronted Grams about the financial situation, but each time a look at her grandmother stopped her. Grams looked so tired. So old.

She'd never thought of her grandmother as needing someone to take care of her. Now she'd have to, even though she suspected Grams wouldn't take kindly to any suggestion that she couldn't manage her own affairs.

Well, she'd let the topic ride until tomorrow, at least. Maybe by then she'd have come up with some tactful way of approaching the subject and Grams would, she hoped, have had a decent night's sleep.

She opened her laptop. In an instant she was completely engrossed in work.

Finally the numbers began to blur on the screen. She got up, stretching, and walked to the window. Full dark had settled in, and her attention had been so focused on the computer screen that she hadn't even noticed. Maybe she'd been trying to shut out the human problems that she found so much more difficult to deal with than figures.

Her eyes gradually grew accustomed to the darkness. She could make out the pond now, the forsythia bushes along it, and the pale line that was the flagstone path.

She stiffened. There—by the toolshed. That wasn't a bush—it was a person. She froze, watching the faint gleam of a shielded light cross the door of the shed.

He was breaking in. She whirled, racing out of the room and across the hall to burst in on her grandmother, who sat up in bed with a Bible on her lap. Barney jumped up, ears pricking.

"Andrea, what—"

"There's someone prowling around by the toolshed. Call the police and alert Cal. I'm going to turn the outside lights on."

She could hear Grams protesting as she bolted down the stairs, the dog at her heels.

FOUR

Andrea reached the back door and slapped the switch that controlled the outside lights. They sprang up instantly, bathing the area with soft illumination. The yellow glow was probably intentional on Rachel's part. It fit well with the style of the two-and-a-half-century-old building, but at the moment, Andrea would rather have harsh fluorescents that lit up every shadowy corner.

She peered through the glass pane in the door, shivering a little. The dog, pressing against her leg, trembled, too, probably eager to get outside and chase whatever lay in the shadows.

The flowers were mere shapes that moved restlessly in the breeze, as if they sensed something wrong. She strained to see beyond the patio. There was the pale outline of the pond, and beyond it nothing but angular shadows.

She heard a step at the top of the stairs behind her.

"I tried Cal, but there was no answer. Perhaps it's him you saw outside."

If so, she was going to feel like an idiot for overreacting. "Does he usually look around the grounds at night?" He'd mentioned looking for the prowler, and after their conversation, that seemed likely. The tension eased.

"Sometimes. But I called the police anyway. Now, don't start worrying about it." Grams seemed to be reading her mind. "I'd rather be safe than sorry."

But she couldn't help the chagrin she felt. City-dweller, jumping to conclusions at the slightest thing.

Well, if so, Cal was the one who'd spooked her, with his talk of prowlers and thieves. He and Uncle Nick had done the job between them.

A heavy flashlight hung on the hook next to the back door, just where Grandfather had always kept one. Clutching the collar of the excited dog, she opened the door, then reached up and took the flashlight.

"Andrea, don't go out," Grams said. "I'm sure it's fine, but wait for the police. Or Cal. He'll come to the house when he sees all the lights on."

Obviously Grams wasn't worried. A little embarrassing, to have her elderly grandmother reassuring her.

"I'll just step outside and flash the light around. See if I can spot Cal. Or anyone."

The dog surged forward, tail waving, apparently welcoming this change in his usual routine. Did the waving tail indicate he sensed a friend?

She edged down the two steps to the patio, lifting the flashlight to probe the shadows beyond the pond. Even as she did, the wail of sirens pierced the night.

She must have relaxed her grip at the sound, because Barney pulled free and darted off toward the lane, letting out an excited bark. Turning, she caught a glimpse of what might be a dark figure. Her heart jolted. She swung the light toward it, but the beam didn't reach far enough to show her anything suspicious.

The dog barked again, a high, excited yip.

If it had been an intruder, he'd be thoroughly scared away by the dog, the lights and the sirens. The lane led to the road—if he went that way, he might run straight into the arms of the police, although he'd hardly be so foolish.

She swung the light back toward the shed where she'd first glimpsed the figure. Everything was still. Reassured by the wail of the police car as it turned in the drive, she crossed the patio, flashing the light around. Nothing seemed to be disturbed.

Cal had said the outbuildings were stuffed to the rafters with furniture. She focused the flashlight on the toolshed. Nothing moved now. The shed was a dark rectangle, with a darker rectangle for the door.

She frowned, trying to pick out details in the shaft of light. Memory provided her with an image of the door as she'd seen it earlier, and tension trailed along her nerves. There had been a padlock on the door. If it was open, someone had been breaking in.

She glanced toward the house. Grams stood in the lighted doorway, peering out.

"Grams, I'm going to check the toolshed. Please don't come out."

"Be careful." Grams sounded a little shaky.

"I will. But if anyone was here, he's long gone by now." She called the words back over her shoulder, moving toward the shed. If something had been stolen on her second night here, she was going to feel responsible.

A mental list began to take shape. Get better outdoor lighting, whether it enhanced the ambience or not. Ask the police to make a regular swing by the property. New locks on any building that held something of value. If what Cal had said was right, that could be any of the half-dozen or more outbuildings.

Every building should be properly inventoried. If it hadn't been done when her grandfather died, it should be done as soon as possible.

Grams and Rachel hadn't thought of that—their minds didn't work that way, as Cal had pointed out. Hers did. He hadn't intended a compliment, but she considered her organizational skills an asset. If her mother had been a bit more meticulous, maybe they wouldn't have spent so much time evading the bill collectors.

She shook that thought off, because remembering those days gave her a queasy feeling in her stomach and an inclination to check her bank balance, just to be sure she was all right.

Hardly surprising. Other children's bogeymen had been monsters and snakes. Hers had been collection agencies.

"Barney! Come, Barney." Her grandmother's voice fluted over the dark garden.

She glanced back the way she'd come to see the dog's pale coat as he bounded toward Grams. Apparently Barney hadn't been in time to take a piece out of their intruder.

Ahead of her, the entrance to the toolshed yawned open, sending a faint shiver of fear across her skin. She hadn't been imagining things. Someone had been here.

A few steps took her to the shed door. With a vague thought of fingerprints, she didn't touch it. She'd shine the light inside, that's all. There was no way of knowing if anything was missing, but at least she could see if it looked disturbed. And get an idea of what she had to deal with.

She leaned forward, light piercing the darkness, giving her a jumbled view of wooden pieces—straight chairs, tables, shelves, even an old icebox, jammed on top of each other...

A quick impression of movement, a dark figure. She couldn't react, couldn't even scream as a hand shot out, shoving her into the toolshed.

She barreled into the edge of a table, cracking her head on something above it. Stars showered through the darkness. She stumbled, hitting the floor just as the door banged shut.

For an instant dizziness engulfed her, followed by a wave of sheer, uncontrollable panic. She was shut in, she was alone in the dark—

She bolted to her feet, grabbed at the door, fumbling for a handle, a latch. "Let me out!"

Shout, don't cry, don't let yourself cry or the panic will take over.

"Help! Help me!"

The door jerked open, and she hurtled out. She caught back a sob, her hands closing on the soft fabric of a shirt and solid muscle. She knew him by instinct before she could see him.

"Cal—there was someone here. Did you see him?"

He pulled her clear of the door and slammed it shut. "Are you okay?"

"Yes." They'd had this exchange before, hadn't they? "I'm fine. Did you see him?"

"I saw him." He sounded grim. "Not enough to describe him, unfortunately. You?"

She shook her head. "Just a blur of movement when he pushed me into the shed. I'm sorry."

He grunted, a frustrated sound. "I was following him. If you hadn't sounded the alarm, I might have caught him."

Cal shook his head in response to Katherine's repeated offer of another cup of chamomile tea. "No, thanks, I've had plenty." One cup of the pale brew was surely enough to satisfy the demands of politeness.

"I think that's everything we need." The young township cop sat awkwardly at the kitchen table, looking half-afraid to touch the delicate Haviland cup and saucer that sat in front of him.

"Do you think you'll catch the thief?" Katherine was as much at ease in her kitchen, wearing a fuzzy red bathrobe, as if she sat in the parlor.

"That might be too much to expect, Grams." Andrea spoke before the cop could come up with an answer. "None of us actually saw the man, and he didn't take anything, as far as we know."

While the cop's attitude toward Katherine was one of respect bordering on awe, the glance he turned on Andrea was simply admiration.

Cal understood. Even casual and disheveled, wearing jeans and a loose blue shirt, Andrea was cool and elegant. And frosty, when she looked at him. Apparently his comment about her interfering with his pursuit of the intruder still rankled.

"I'd best be on my way, ma'am." The cop rose, settling his uniform cap over a thatch of straw-colored hair as he headed for the back door. "We'll do the best we can to keep an eye on the place."

"Thank you, Officer." Katherine was graciousness itself. "We appreciate that."

Once the door closed behind him, Cal shook his head. "That won't be often enough. The township cops have too much territory to cover and too few men. What you need out there is better lighting."

"That's just what I was thinking." Once again Andrea looked faintly surprised to find herself agreeing with him. "I'll call about it in the morning."

"I don't think that's necessary. If we leave on the lights we have, that should suffice." Katherine set a cup and saucer in the sink, the china chattering against itself, betraying her emotion.

"I can install them," he said, knowing she was probably worrying about the cost, "if Andrea gets the fixtures."

Andrea nodded. "Of course." Her gaze crossed his, and he knew they were thinking the same thing. "It'll be my contribution to the renovations."

"I don't want you to spend your money on this." Katherine's eyes darkened with distress. "After all, you didn't think the inn was a good idea."

She probably still didn't, but she managed a smile. "I have to take part. The sign does say The Three Sisters Inn, after all." She put her arm around her grandmother's waist and urged her toward the stairs. "You go up to bed, Grams. I'll just talk to Cal about the lights, and then I'll see him out."

"Thank you, dear." Katherine patted her cheek, and then came over to touch him lightly on the shoulder. "And you, Cal. I don't know what we'd have done without you tonight."

"No problem," he said easily. "Have a good night's sleep."

She nodded. "Come, Barney." The dog padded obediently after her. "That's my good, brave dog," she crooned, starting up the stairs. "You were so clever to chase the bad man away."

He waited until he heard her door close to shake his head. "I've never been overly impressed with Barney's intelligence, and tonight confirmed that. He ran to me, recognizing a friend, instead of chasing the prowler."

Andrea frowned. "Even if he's not the brightest dog in the world, you'd think he'd go after a stranger."

That thought had occurred to him, too, but he didn't see anything to be gained by pursuing it now. If this was the same person who'd broken into several farmhouses, he could be someone local, even someone who'd been to the house before.

She sat down across from him, apparently willing to forget her annoyance in the need to talk with someone. "Do you think he was planning to steal something tonight, or just checking things out for a future visit?"

"I'm not sure." He balanced the silver teaspoon on his finger. Silver, good china, antiques—there was plenty here to tempt a thief. "He may have wanted to see where the best stuff was. I would expect him to come with a truck of some sort if he planned to haul away any antiques. Pennsylvania German pieces tend to be pretty hefty, to say the least."

"I suppose you're right. He did break the lock, though."

"Meaning he wouldn't have done that unless he planned to take something? I'm not sure you're right. He couldn't know what was there unless he got in to have a look around."

"I guess." She ran her hands through the silky strands of blond hair in a gesture of frustration. "I don't even know what's in the shed. How could they get away without a proper inventory when my grandfather died?" She sounded slightly outraged, as if lack of the right paperwork was a moral failing.

"Maybe that's a good job for you." It would keep her busy, anyway.

"I can't imagine how long that would take. More time than I have, at any rate. But I'll call a locksmith and have decent locks put on all those buildings."

A slight feeling of sympathy surprised him. Andrea was trying to do the right thing for her grandmother, even if she didn't agree with her decisions.

"I can put new locks on. We'll get them when we go for the light fixtures tomorrow."

"We?" Her eyebrows lifted.

"We. Unless you're well-informed as to the best type of light fixtures and locks to use."

Her eyes narrowed, and he could almost see her trying to pigeonhole him. "I thought you were a carpenter, not a handyman."

"I know a little about a lot of useful things."

"In that case, I'm surprised you didn't offer to do the lights and the locks before," she said tartly. "Since you were so quick to warn me about the danger."

"I did. Numerous times." He rose, carrying his cup and saucer to the sink. "Katherine always turned me down. She held tightly to the illusion that this place was still safe. After tonight, I don't think that's an issue, sadly. She'll let us do it."

"You really don't need to help." Andrea's chair scraped as she shoved it in, the only sound in the room other than the ticktock of the ornate Black Forest mantel clock. "I'm sure my grandmother appreciates your offer, but I can hire someone. I'll pay—"

He swung around, annoyed that she thought this was about money. "I said I'd do it."

"It's my responsibility." That stubborn jaw was very much in evidence. "Why should you be involved?"

"Because I live here, too. Because your grandmother and your sister have both been kind to me."

Because they can accept me as I am, without needing a dossier on my past.

Her hands moved, palms up, in a gesture of surrender. "All right, then. If you feel that way about it, I guess we'd better head out to the hardware store tomorrow."

"Fine." He strode toward the door and pulled it open. "Be sure you lock this behind me."

"You don't need to remind me of that." The ghost of a smile touched her lips as she came to the door and reached for the dead bolt. "I'm a city-dweller, remember? Locking up is second nature to me."

She stood close in the dim light, with the half-opened door between them like a wedge. Her face looked softer in the shadows, more vulnerable.

The way it had looked when she'd catapulted out of the shed practically into his arms. He'd felt her heart racing in the instant she'd pressed against him. She'd been panic-stricken, although she was hardly likely to admit that to him.

"Katherine could use a few street smarts. But I can't see her changing at this time of her life, so we'll have to take care of it for her."

She nodded, but he thought there was still a question in her eyes. About him. She wasn't like Katherine and Rachel in that regard. She didn't accept anyone at face value.

No, if Andrea stuck around for long, she'd be trying to find out more about him. She'd have to know, just so she could fit him into her neat classification system. And if she did, it would only raise more questions in her mind. Why would a rising young attorney in a prestigious firm throw it all over after winning the case of his career? She'd want to know the answer.

She wouldn't. No one here knew but him. His conscience would never let him forget the mistake he'd made in his rush to get ahead, or the child his stupidity had returned to an abusive father. It had cost his career to right that wrong, and he didn't figure he was finished paying yet. But that wasn't Andrea's business.

"Good night." His fingers brushed hers lightly as he grasped the door to pull it shut behind him. "Pleasant dreams."

* * *

"So basically it was much ado about nothing." Andrea gave Rachel her most reassuring smile the next morning. "Really. Stop looking so worried."

Of course Rachel couldn't help it, tethered as she was to a wheelchair by the two heavy casts. The chair was parked by the window, but she didn't look as if she'd been enjoying the view of the hospital's helipad.

"I knew we should have taken more security measures, especially after thieves broke into the Bauman farmhouse and vandals knocked over some of the gravestones in the church cemetery." She brushed a soft brown curl behind her ear with a quick gesture, brow crinkled. "But Grams still thinks this place is as safe as it was fifty years ago, and anyway, she said—" She stopped abruptly, guilt plainly written on her face.

"Relax, Rachel. I talked to Uncle Nick. I know about Grams's finances."

Rachel blinked. "He told you?"

"Yes. What I want to know is, why didn't you tell me?" She forced the hurt out of her voice.

Discomfort made her sister move restlessly in the wheelchair. "You know Grams. She's proud. The only reason I found out was because I happened to be visiting when she hit a low point."

"So you came up with the idea of starting the bed-and-breakfast to help her." How disapproving did she sound? Apparently some, because Rachel's gaze slid away from hers.

"It seems like a good use for the house. Nobody needs a huge place like that just to live in."

"Exactly." She sat down in the vinyl padded chair that was all the room offered for a visitor, turning it to face Rachel. "So wouldn't Grams be better off to sell? The place is way too big for her, and I don't think she should have the worry of starting a business at this time of life."

"You don't understand." Rachel straightened, eyes flashing. "Grams loves that place. Unger House has been her home for fifty years. How can you act as if it would be easy for her to give it up?"

That was as much anger as she'd seen from Rachel since Caroline stole her boyfriend in tenth grade. She leaned forward, resting her hand on her sister's.

"I know it wouldn't be easy, but doesn't that point come to everyone? When people get older, they usually have to move into a place that's more manageable. I'm sure Grams understands that."

Rachel's expression was unusually stubborn. "She's not ready for that. Besides, she always assumed there'd be family to take over Unger House one day. Us."

That was like a blow to the stomach. "She—why would she think that? It's been years since we left."

"Not that long, as Grams sees it." Rachel tilted her head, surveying Andrea with an expression that suggested she just didn't get it. "You're the one who had the most time here. I'd think you'd have lots of good memories."

"Good memories?" Something hardened in her. "What I remember is being dragged out of the house with half our belongings, Caro screaming, Grams crying, and Grandfather standing there like a statue. As if he didn't care."

"Oh, honey." Rachel patted her hand as if she was the one who needed comfort. "I know how bad that was, but can't you think about all the good times, instead? We were happy here once."

She jerked her feelings back under control, shoving the images from that day behind a closed door. In her ordinary life, she never let them out. Here, she'd been tripping over them every other minute, it seemed.

"You've always been the peacemaker, Rachel, trying to make everyone else feel good." Lucky Rachel had the gift of being able to separate out the bad stuff and remember only the happy times. She didn't, it seemed.

"There were lots of good things," Rachel insisted. "Remember the time the power went off in the big snowstorm, and Eli and Levi Zook brought the horse and sleigh and took us for a ride over the fields to their place? Having the power go off wasn't a problem for them, since they don't depend on it anyway."

"I remember." She couldn't help a smile. "Caroline tried to teach Eli and Emma's kids how to do the hokey-pokey. I don't think they appreciated it."

"The point is that if Grams wants to stay at Unger House, I'm ready to help her do it. The bed-and-breakfast seemed like the logical answer." She rubbed the wrinkle that formed between her brows. "My getting hurt wasn't part of the plan, but I still think if they'd let me go home, we could work it out. Emma's a good cook, and if I'm there to supervise—"

"Absolutely not." That was one thing she was sure of in this situation. "I've talked to the doctors. You need rest, healing and therapy, in that order. No coming home until they give the okay."

Rachel looked at her steadily. "If I do that, how is Grams going to get the inn ready to open? She can't do it herself. Just making all the decisions, let alone the work—"

"She won't be doing it by herself." She'd reached the point she'd probably known all along she would. This wasn't her dream, but she couldn't let her family down. "I'll stay and do my best to get the inn off the ground."

She could only hope that she wouldn't have to sacrifice her job in order to do it.

FIVE

Andrea hurried through the center hallway toward the rear of the house, pausing in the small room that had been first a summer kitchen, then later a playroom for her and her sisters. They'd loved the huge fireplace, big enough to roast a whole side of beef. They'd pretended they were Cinderella, sweeping the hearth. Come to think of it, Caroline had always gotten to play Cinderella. She'd been the wicked stepmother.

That was how Rachel had made her feel at her suggestion of selling Unger House—like the wicked stepmother. That stung, with its implication that Rachel cared more, understood more, than she did. She still thought selling was the logical solution, but she was smart enough to know when a plan, logical or not, didn't stand a chance of success.

So she was heading to the hardware store with Cal, putting off the two things she was least eager to do today. Confronting her grandmother about the financial situation, for one. And then telling her boss she needed a leave of absence. Knowing him, she'd be lucky if he didn't simply give her a choice—her family or her job.

Something winced inside her at that. She deserved that promotion. She'd worked hard for it, sacrificing everything else in her drive to succeed. It wasn't fair that she might lose it now.

She pushed through the swinging door to the kitchen. "Emma, do you need anything—"

She stopped, nerves jumping. Emma was not in sight, but a man stood with his back to her—tall, broad, black pants and a black jacket, his hand in a drawer of the hutch that held the everyday china.

"What are you doing?" The edge to her voice was put there by fear, but she wouldn't give in to the feeling. Wouldn't let herself think about the dark figure that had shoved her into the toolshed. It was broad daylight now, and she wasn't afraid.

The man froze, then turned slowly toward her. It was like watching a mountain move. His face became visible, and something jolted inside her. The face was oddly unformed, as if a sculptor had started working on it and then walked away, uninterested in finishing. Blue eyes, rounded cheeks like a child's...

Emma hurried in from the pantry, her white apron fluttering, eyes worried behind wire-rimmed glasses. "What are you doing, Levi? You remember Andrea, don't you?"

"I remember him." Andrea tried to soften her embarrassment with a smile. Of course. She should have recognized him at once. Emma's oldest son was two years older than she was chronologically. Mentally, he was still the child he'd been long ago. "How are you, Levi?"

"Say good day," Emma prompted, but he just shook his head, taking a step back until he bumped the hutch.

"That's all right," Andrea said, trying to smooth over the uncomfortable moment. "Maybe later Levi will want to talk to me."

Levi's round blue eyes filled with tears. With an incoherent sound, he turned and ran from the kitchen, the screen door slamming behind him.

She could kick herself. "I'm so sorry." She turned to Emma. "I didn't mean to upset him that way."

"He will be fine." Emma didn't seem upset. "He just needs time to get used to new people."

"Doesn't he remember me?" Her own childhood memories were flooding back faster and faster, no matter how much she tried to block them out.

Emma shook her head. "He knows you, for sure. He just doesn't understand about how people change. I'll tell him a couple of times about how you're Andrea all grown-up. He'll be fine."

Certainly Emma didn't seem worried about the incident. Her oval face, innocent of makeup, was as serene as always. Whatever grief she'd endured over Levi's condition had long ago been accepted as God's will, the way she'd accept a lightning strike that hit the barn or a bumper crop of tomatoes to take to market as God's will.

Andrea went to press her cheek against Emma's, affection surging within her. Maybe she'd be a better person if she had a little of that kind of acceptance.

"Well, you tell Levi I was happy to see him, anyway." She dismissed that flare of apprehension that had gripped her when she'd seen him at the hutch. "Rachel was just reminding me of the big snowstorm, when we came to your house in the sleigh. Levi helped his father drive the horses, I remember."

"Ach, I will tell him." Emma beamed at the reminiscence, rubbing her hands on the full skirt of her plain, wine-colored dress. "He will remember that, he will."

They'd all played together then—Amish and English—it hadn't mattered to the children. Emma's oldest daughter, Sarah, had been her exact age. She'd longed go to school with Sarah in the simple white school-house down the road, instead of getting on the yellow school bus for the trip to the consolidated elementary.

"How is Sarah? Married, I know from my grand-mother."

"Married with six young ones of her own, and training to be a midwife, besides." Emma's pride was manifest, though she'd never admit it.

"Please greet her for me, too." They'd all grown and gone their separate ways. Only Levi had remained, a child still, but in a man's body. "I'm going to the hardware store with Cal to get some new lights and locks. I wondered if you needed anything."

Emma's plump face paled. "Locks? Why? Has something happened?"

She'd assumed Grams would have mentioned it, but possibly they hadn't had a chance to talk before Grams set off for the hospital.

"We had a prowler last night." She didn't want to alarm Emma, but surely it was better that she know. "He tried to get into the old toolshed."

"Did you—did you get a look at this person?" Emma's hands twisted together under her apron.

She shook her head, sorry now that she'd mentioned it. She didn't want to distress Emma. Probably she, like Grams, still thought of this area as perfectly safe.

"He ran away when he heard the dog and the sirens." Maybe it was just as well not to mention her closer encounter with the man. "We're going to put up brighter lighting in the grounds. Hopefully that will keep any troublemakers away."

"*Ja.*" Emma pulled open the door under the sink, peering inside. "*Ja,* maybe it will. I can't think of anything that I need from the store."

Andrea hesitated a moment, studying the tense lines of Emma's shoulders under the dark dress, the averted face. The thought of a prowler had upset her more than expected, but Andrea didn't know what to do to ease her mind.

"Don't worry about it, please, Emma. I'm sure the lights will solve the problem. And if you're concerned about walking back and forth to the farm, I'd be happy to drive you."

"No, no." Emma whisked that offer away with a sweeping gesture. "I am fine. No one will bother me."

There didn't seem to be anything else to say, but Andrea frowned as she walked to the door. They couldn't afford to have Emma upset. Grams needed her more than she ever had.

They both did, if they were really going to open the inn on time, and though she could hardly believe it of herself, it seemed she was committed to this crazy venture.

* * *

From his perch on the stone wall that wound along the patio, Cal watched the black-clad figure vanish from sight around the barn. He and Levi had reached the point that Levi would sometimes speak to him, but today he'd rushed past without a word. Something had upset him, obviously.

Cal latched his hands around his knee. Andrea had said she'd meet him, and he'd guess she was the type to be on time. So he'd come a bit early, not wanting to give her a reason to say he'd kept her waiting.

Sure enough, she hurried out the back door, checking her watch as she did. She looked up, saw him and came toward him at a more deliberate pace.

"Sorry. Have you been waiting?"

"Only for a couple of minutes." He got up leisurely. "I saw Levi come running out."

"I suppose you think I frightened him."

He held both hands up in a gesture of surrender. "Peace. That wasn't aimed at you. I know how shy he is. It's taken months to get him to the point of nodding at me."

A faint flush touched her cheeks. "I guess that did sound pretty defensive, didn't it? I was startled that Levi didn't seem to remember me."

He fell into step beside her as they walked toward the stone garage that had started life as a stable. "I take it you knew him when you were children."

What had she been like as a child? Flax hair in braids, he supposed, probably bossing the others around because she was the oldest.

She nodded, those green eyes seeming fixed on something far away. "They were our neighbors. Emma's daughter Sarah was my closest friend." She shook her head. "It seems odd now, when I think of it. As if it happened in a different world."

That, he thought, was the most unguarded thing she'd said to him yet. "I suppose it was, in a way. Childhood, I mean."

"The differences didn't seem so great to a child. We drove my grandfather crazy by talking in the low German dialect the Zook children used at home."

"He didn't like that?" He gestured her toward the truck. When she hesitated, he opened the passenger door for her. "We may as well take this. Rachel's compact doesn't have much trunk room."

She nodded, climbing in. When he slid behind the wheel, she went on as if the interruption hadn't happened.

"I'm not really sure why he objected. His family was what the Amish call 'fancy' German, just as they call themselves the 'plain folk.'" She shrugged. "He didn't insist—maybe he knew that would just make us more determined. Or maybe he saw that Emma's family was good for us." Some faint shadow crossed her face at that.

"Sounds as if you and your sisters had a good childhood here," he said lightly. "I was an urban kid, myself. Never saw a real cow until I was twelve."

"Good?" Again that shadow. "Yes, I guess. Until it ended."

He glanced toward her. "Ended sounds rather final."

She blinked, and he could almost see her realizing that she'd said more to him than she'd intended. She shrugged, seeming to try for a casual movement.

"Everyone outgrows being a kid. Can we get what we need at Clymer's Hardware, or do we have to go farther?"

Obviously the subject was closed. Maybe only the encounter with Levi had opened her that much. Something had happened to put a period to that innocent time, maybe the same thing that had kept her away from here for so long. Whatever it was, she wasn't going to tell him.

So be it. He wouldn't pry, any more than he wanted someone prying into his life. "Clymer's. I know your grandmother likes to use local businesses if she can."

"Fine."

He pulled into the lot next to the frame building with old-fashioned gilt lettering on the glass windows. He loved going into the village hardware store. It was nice to be in a place where people knew your name, as the song said.

Clymer's was as much a center for male gossip as the grocery store was for female gossip, in the way of small towns. Here they'd be talking about who needed new fencing and how the alfalfa was coming along.

Andrea slid out quickly, and he followed her to the door. She stepped inside, pausing as if getting her bearings.

"Lighting fixtures are in the back." He nodded toward the aisle.

Detouring around kegs of nails and the coil of rope that hung handy to be measured off, they headed back to where sample fixtures hung, gleaming palely in the daylight. Ted Clymer looked up from the counter where he was working a crossword puzzle and raised a hand in greeting. Ted seemed to figure if his customers needed any help, they'd ask for it. Otherwise, he left them alone.

Andrea came to a halt in the midst of racks of light fixtures. She turned toward him. "I'm not too proud to admit when I'm out of my depth. What do you think we need?"

Since he'd already decided, he was relieved that they weren't going to argue about it. He chose two brands and set the boxes in front of her. "Either one of these would do the job."

"Which do you recommend?"

He put his hand on the more expensive brand. "This will cost more to begin with, but it's higher rated. Still, the other one will serve."

She shook her head decisively. "I don't want to worry that they'll have to be replaced in a couple of years. How many do you think we need to cover the area?"

"I'd say six would do it." He glanced at the racks. "Ted doesn't have that many out, but he probably has more in the back."

She picked up the box. "I'll ask him to get them while you're picking out the locks." Her smile flickered. "You don't need to ask my opinion. Just get what you think will work best."

So apparently Andrea trusted him in that, at least, and she wasn't grudging the money spent on something her grandmother needed. He watched her walk toward the counter. Even in khaki pants and a fitted denim jacket, she had just enough of an urban flair to let you know she didn't belong here.

Too bad. Because Katherine would like having her around, not because it mattered to him.

It took a few minutes to find locks that satisfied him. Nothing would keep out a really determined thief, but these would discourage anyone who was looking for a lock that could be popped quickly and quietly.

He headed back to the counter, his hands full, but checked when he saw the person who stood next to Andrea, talking away as if they were old friends. Margaret Allen. He'd be willing to bet that no legitimate errand had brought her into the hardware store. It was far more likely that she'd spotted them from across the street and decided to check up on the competition.

He approached and dropped the locks on the counter, their clatter interrupting the conversation. "That's it for us, Ted. Ring us up."

He turned, forcing a smile. "Hello, Margaret. How's business?"

She returned the smile with one that had syrup oozing off it. Margaret looked, he always thought, like a well-fed, self-satisfied cat, and never so much as when she was asserting her position as the owner of the finest inn in the county. Just how far would she go to maintain that status? The question had begun pricking at the back of his mind lately.

"How nice to see you, Cal. I was just telling Andrea how wonderful it is of her to come and help her grandmother at such a sad time. Poor Rachel. I'm afraid all their visions of starting a bed-and-breakfast will be lost. Still, I always say that every cloud has a silver lining, and I'm sure in the end, this disappointment will be for the best. Don't you agree, Andrea?"

Andrea looked a little dazed at the flood of saccharine. "Yes, I mean—"

"We have to go." He handed Andrea the credit card Ted had been patiently holding out. "Lots to do. Nice seeing you, Margaret." He scooped up boxes, handing the bag containing the locks to Andrea, and nudged her toward the door.

She shot him an annoyed look. "I'm glad to have met you, Ms. Allen. I'll tell my sister you asked about her."

They reached the pickup, and he started loading fixtures quickly, not having any desire to hang around for another interrogation from Margaret.

Andrea dropped the bag with the locks into the pickup bed. "You didn't have to be rude to that poor woman. She was just expressing her concern."

"Right." He shook his head. "That was Margaret Allen." He pointed to the Georgian mansion across the street with its twin weeping willows overhanging the wrought iron fence. "That Margaret Allen, owner of The Willows bed-and-breakfast."

"She said she was a friend of my grandmother's." Andrea climbed in, frowning at him as he got behind the wheel. "Maybe she did gush a bit, but I'm sure she meant well."

"A bit?" He lifted an eyebrow. "You looked as if you were drowning in it."

Her lips twitched. "Just because she runs another B and B, that doesn't make her the enemy."

"In her mind, it does. Believe me. She takes pride in having the only inn in Churchville, and she doesn't like to share the limelight, or the tourist dollars, with anyone." He pulled out onto Main Street for the short drive home.

"Surely there's enough tourist trade to go around."

He shrugged. "Ask Rachel, if you don't believe me. She's the one who's had to deal with her. The other B and B operators in the county have been supportive, by and large, but Margaret created one problem after another."

"What could she do? Surely you don't think she was our prowler."

That was a thought that hadn't occurred to him, and he filed it for future consideration. "I don't see her wandering around in the dark, no, but she has played dirty. Complaints to the township zoning board, complaints to the tourist bureau, complaints to the bed-and-breakfast owners association. All couched in such sickeningly sweet language you'd think she was doing them a favor by putting up roadblocks."

"Maybe she was." It was said so softly he almost missed it.

"Is that what you'll tell your grandmother when you bail and leave them on their own?" The edge in his voice startled him. He hadn't meant to say that.

He felt Andrea's gaze on him and half expected an explosion. He didn't get it.

"Think what you like." Her tone dismissed him, as if he were no more important in the scheme of things than the barn cat. "But as a matter of fact, I'm not leaving. I'm staying until I can be sure that my grand-mother and sister are all right."

It silenced him for a moment. "What about your job?"

Her fingers clenched in her lap. "I don't know. Talking to my boss is a pleasure I haven't had yet."

"I'm sorry. I hope he understands."

"So do I." Her fingers tightened until her knuckles were white.

"It means that much to you?"

"Yes. It does." She clipped off the words, as if he didn't have the right to know why.

She was willing to sacrifice something that was im-portant to her for the sake of someone else. The few people who knew the truth about him might say he'd done the same, but he'd done it as much for himself as for anyone else, because he'd known he couldn't live with himself if he hadn't.

It had brought him unexpected benefits in the long run—helped him to know what he wanted from life, brought him to faith. Still, he couldn't assume that would be the result for Andrea's sacrifice.

"I hope it works out for you, Andrea. Really."

He glanced across the confines of the front seat at her. There was something startled, a little wary, in her eyes. As if she wasn't sure whether she believed him. Or maybe as if it mattered what he thought.

SIX

Andrea sat in the room she still thought of as her grandfather's library that afternoon, frowning over the rather sketchy records Rachel seemed to be keeping on the inn's start-up. Sketchy didn't cover it. Surely Rachel had better records than this. If not, they were in more trouble than she'd imagined.

She flipped through the file folder, her frustration growing. Hadn't Rachel been saving receipts, at least? Grams might know if she had records elsewhere. Maybe, like Grandfather, she preferred to do it all by hand, although he had been far more organized than this.

Grandfather's tall green ledgers had been a fixture of their childhood. Presumably the insurance and real estate business he'd shared with Uncle Nick had long since been computerized, but she'd always associate her grandfather with those meticulously handwritten ledgers. She glanced at the shelf where they'd once stood in a neat row, but it was now occupied by a welter of tourist brochures and bed-and-breakfast books. Rachel must have moved them.

The front door closed, and Barney gave the excited

yelp that meant the center of his existence had returned. The scrabble of his nails on the plank floor was followed by the crooning voice Grams reserved for him. Andrea had to smile. She couldn't imagine her dignified grandmother talking baby talk to any other creature but Barney.

"Andrea?" Her grandmother came in, followed by the excited dog. "Good, you're here. I'd like to speak with you."

The determined set to Grams's jaw told her that any questions about Rachel's record-keeping would have to wait. Grams clearly had an agenda of her own.

Andrea swung the leather swivel chair around so that she faced the wingback tapestry chair that was Grams's favorite. The desk chair had been Grandfather's. It was too big for Andrea, and she felt slightly uncomfortable in it, as if she sat in the boss's chair without permission.

"How's Rachel? Did you tell her I'll come to see her this evening?"

Grams sat down, her expression lightening a little. "I thought she seemed a bit stronger today. She didn't look quite so pale. Nick had been in with a lovely arrangement of roses, and Pastor Hartman came just as I was leaving."

"That's good." Good that Rachel seemed better, and good that she was having other company. Perhaps that would keep Grams from feeling guilty if she couldn't be there every minute.

"Yes." Grams fondled the dog's ears for a moment, frowning a little. "I understand from Rachel that you know about my financial situation. That James Bendick told you."

That must really rankle, or Grams would be using the nickname that she'd adopted along with the children. "Please don't blame Uncle Nick, Grams. I'd already guessed some of it, and I made him tell me what was going on."

That didn't seem to have the desired effect. Grams still looked severe. "Nevertheless, he doesn't have the right to discuss my affairs without my permission. I'll have to speak to him about it."

The threat to be spoken to by Grams had been such a part of her childhood that it almost made her smile. *Andrea Katherine, do I have to speak to you?* The words echoed from the past.

Grams was taking this too seriously for smiling, however, and they had to discuss the situation, whether Grams wanted to confide in her or not.

"Uncle Nick probably thought I'd heard it already, from you. Which I should have. Why on earth didn't you tell me about the financial problems? You must know I'd help any way I can."

Grams turned her face away, and for a moment Andrea thought she wasn't going to answer. Then she realized that her grandmother was looking at the portrait of Grandfather that hung over the mantelpiece on the other side of the room.

"I didn't want you to think ill of your grandfather. Or any more than you already do."

The words were spoken so softly that it took a moment for them to register. And when they did, Andrea felt a flush rise on her cheeks. "I don't know what you mean."

Grams looked at her then, her blue eyes chiding. "Yes, you do, Andrea. You've never forgiven him for the quarrel with your mother."

It was like being slapped. She'd never dreamed that Grams guessed her feelings. Obviously she hadn't been as good at hiding them as she'd thought. She took a breath, trying to compose herself. She couldn't let whatever lingering resentment she had affect what she did now.

"It was a long time ago, Grams. What's important is what's going on now."

Her grandmother shook her head slowly, delicate silver earrings echoing the movement. "The past is always important, Andrea. Your grandfather was a good man. He gave me a comfortable life, and I won't hear a word against him just because he made a few wrong business decisions."

It must have been more than a few, some practical part of her mind commented, but she shooed away the thought. She had to help Grams, but she'd hoped to steer clear of Grandfather's mistakes, knowing that would hurt her.

"He loved you very much, Grams."

For the first time since her return, Andrea stared directly at the portrait. Her grandfather's image stared back—blue eyes as piercing as she remembered, the planes of his face still strong even when the painting was done, to commemorate Grandfather's retirement from the state legislature at sixty-five. He looked like a man you could count on.

But he also looked stubborn. In the case of his daughter, the stiff-necked stubbornness had won out over any other consideration, including his grandchildren.

"He loved you, too, dear. I know you find that hard to believe, but he did."

"He let her take us away." The voice of her childhood popped out before she could censor it.

Grams reached out to grasp her hand. "He couldn't stop her. She was your mother." She shook her head. "I know you think he could have mended things with her, but you must be old enough now to see how it was. He was proud, and your mother—well, she was willful. They could never stop the quarrel long enough to admit they loved each other."

Willful, reckless, lavish with both affection and temper—yes, she knew what her mother had been like. How had two such solid citizens as her grandparents have produced Lily Unger Hampton? That had to be one of the mysteries of genetics.

"I'm sorry, Grams." To her horror, she felt tears well in her eyes. "I know it hurt you, too." But her grandmother would never know just how bad it had been for her precious grandchildren, at least not if Andrea could help it.

"He grieved when you were taken away." Grams's voice was soft. "You have to believe that, my dear."

Not as much as we did. You were the grown-ups, you and Grandfather, and our mother and father. Why didn't you take better care of us? She wouldn't say that, but she couldn't help feeling it.

Shaking her head, Grams got up. She dipped her hand into a Blue Willow Wedgwood bowl that sat on top of the desk, retrieving the small key. She handed it to Andrea.

"It fits the bottom drawer on the right." She nodded to the massive mahogany desk that had been Grandfather's. "I want you to look inside."

Something in her wanted to rebel, but she couldn't ignore the command in her grandmother's eyes. She bent and unlocked the drawer, pulling it open. Inside were long rectangular boxes, three of them—the sort of archival boxes that preserved documents. The top box had a name, written in black ink in Grandpa's precise lettering. *Andrea.*

She lifted that one, setting it on the desk blotter to remove the lid. Her throat tightened. A picture, drawn by a child's hand, showed two figures—a white-haired man in a navy suit, a child with yellow braids. Before she could dwell on it, she flipped through the rest of the contents.

Report cards, more drawings, dating back to the earliest attempts that were no more than ovals on sticks for figures. Always two of them—grandfather and granddaughter. A handmade valentine, with a lopsided heart pasted onto a white doily, signed with a red crayon. *To Grandfather from your helper.*

She remembered making that one, sitting at the kitchen table, asking Emma to aid with the spelling. Emma, always more adept in German than English, had called Grams in to advise.

Tears stung her eyes, and she fought to keep them from falling. Grams meant well. She was trying to prove that Grandfather had loved her. But if he'd loved her enough to save all these things, why hadn't he loved her enough to do whatever it took to stay a part of her life?

A hot tear splashed on the valentine, and she blotted it away. Yes, Grams meant well. But looking at these reminders didn't make the situation better. Seeing them just made it worse.

Cal rounded the shed on his way to the kitchen. His stride checked abruptly.

Andrea sat on the low stone wall where he'd sat earlier, but she didn't seem to be waiting for anyone. Her cell phone was pressed to her ear, and judging by the expression on her face, the conversation wasn't going well.

He detoured to the walk that circled around, taking him toward the door at a safe distance from her. She'd probably come out to the garden to ensure her privacy, and he wouldn't intrude. But he couldn't prevent a certain amount of curiosity. Was it her boss who put that expression on her face?

Or was it a boyfriend, unhappy at her prolonged absence from the city? That thought generated a surprisingly quick denial. No one had mentioned a boyfriend in Andrea's life, but then again, why would they, to him?

He went on into the kitchen, where he consulted Emma about the exact finish on the piece he was making for her, enjoying prolonging the conversation with a smattering of the low German he'd been attempting to learn. It must still be plenty fractured, judging by her laughter.

That had been one of the things that had surprised him about the Amish when he'd come here. He'd expected, from outward appearances, a dour people, living an uncomfortable life as if it were a duty.

Instead he'd found people who laughed readily and who took as much enjoyment in plowing all day in the sun as they did from sitting on the porch on a summer's evening. Work was not something that was separate from play—all things held their own intrinsic satisfaction, because they were done in obedience to God's will.

It was a lesson he'd been trying to learn, but he suspected that even the trying was self-defeating. He couldn't will himself into finding peace and joy in the everyday things of life. That only happened when he forgot the effort and simply lost himself in what he was doing.

When he went out the back door again, Andrea still sat on the wall. Afternoon sunlight, filtering through the leaves of the giant oak that shaded the patio, turned her silky blond hair to gold. The cell phone lay next to her.

"Hi." He nodded toward the phone. "I didn't want to interrupt you."

"An interruption might have improved the conversation." She grimaced. "No, I take that back. It would just have prolonged it."

"Your boss?" That instinctive sympathy came again.

"He did *not* take the news well. Not even when I assured him I'd keep working on the project from here."

"Did you point out that telecommuting is fast becoming the norm in some businesses?"

"He doesn't think telecommuting will do the trick at this point." She shrugged. "I can't really argue with that. He's probably right."

He propped one foot on the wall and leaned an elbow on his knee. "I assume he finally accepted the inevitable."

"Well, he's not firing me outright, so I suppose that's a good sign. But I suspect my promotion has just moved off into the distant future." Her eyes clouded at that. "I'll do everything I can from here, and my assistant will do what she can, but he'll still be inconvenienced."

"A little inconvenience never hurt anyone. Maybe he'll learn to appreciate you more." He'd like to remove the dismay from her face, but that wasn't within his power.

"Somehow I doubt that."

He sat down next to her. No use pretending he didn't care about her troubles. He couldn't help doing so. "This promotion—it means a lot to you."

A fine line formed between her brows. "It means… security."

Whatever he'd expected her to say—recognition, success, the corner office—it hadn't been that. "Security? That sounds like something I'd expect from a fifty-year-old who's thinking about retirement."

She stiffened. "Security is generally considered a good thing, believe it or not. You don't have to be fifty to think about it. In fact, if you wait until you're fifty, you've put it off too long."

"You're young, smart and, I suspect, talented at what you do." He smiled. "And those are good things, too. They'd be appreciated in plenty of places. Your grandmother says—"

"My grandmother doesn't know anything about business. But you do, don't you?" She swung the full impact of those green eyes on him.

"What makes you say that?" He backtracked, wondering where he'd made a mistake. "I'm just a craftsman."

"You do a pretty good imitation of the country hick from time to time, but that's not who you are, is it?"

He shrugged, almost enjoying parrying with her. She'd never hit on the truth, so what difference did it make?

"I told you I grew up in the city. Any little vestiges of urban sophistication should wear away, in time."

"I'm not talking about growing up in the city." She brushed that away with a wave of her hand. "I'm talking about the corporate mind-set. You understand it too well to be a bystander."

He rose, the enjoyment leaving. He didn't like the turn the conversation was taking. "Hey, I was just trying to be sympathetic."

She studied him for a long moment, her brow furrowed with uncertainty. And he suspected she didn't like being uncertain about anything.

"If that's true, I appreciate it," she said finally. "But I still don't believe you're just a simple craftsman."

His tension eased. She wasn't going to make an issue of it, and even if she did—well, he hadn't committed any crime. At least, not any that the law would call him to book for. Whatever guilt he still carried was between him and God.

"And you're not just a simple financial expert, are you? You're also a granddaughter, a sister, and now an innkeeper."

"Don't remind me." She rubbed at the line between her brows, as if she could rub it away. "I know you won't appreciate how this pains me, but my sister's idea of keeping track of start-up costs consists of throwing receipts in a file."

"She uses a file? I thought my cigar box was pretty sophisticated."

That got a smile, and the line vanished. "You're not going to make me believe that, you know."

"Maybe not." He sobered. "But I hope you'll believe that if anything happens that worries you, you can call me. Any time. I promise I'll answer my phone."

She looked startled. "You mean—but surely with the new lights and the locks, no one would try to break in."

"Sounds a little melodramatic with the sun shining, but I'm still not comfortable about the situation." An ambitious thief might want to see what he could get before the inn opened, filling the place with visitors. And an ambitious rival might think one more incident would be enough to scuttle the inn plans for good. "Just—call me."

Her gaze seemed to weigh him, determining whether and how much to trust him. Finally she nodded.

"All right. If I see or hear anything that concerns me, I'll call you. I promise."

* * *

She'd made a promise she didn't expect she'd have to keep, Andrea thought as she drove home from the hospital that evening. She appreciated Cal's concern, but surely the measures they'd taken would discourage any prospective thief.

Now all she had to worry about was hanging on to her future at work, ensuring Rachel's healing, and getting the inn off and running. Those concerns had actually begun to seem manageable.

The layer of dark clouds that massed on the horizon didn't dampen her optimistic mood. Rachel had looked almost normal tonight, joking about the casts and finally rid of the headache that had dogged her since the accident. Andrea hadn't realized how worried she was about her sister until the weight had lifted with the assurance that Rachel was her buoyant self again.

They had spent nearly two hours going over all of Rachel's plans for the inn, and in spite of her sister's undoubted lack of financial expertise, they probably had a reasonable chance of success. They had a beautiful, historic building in an unmatched setting, and Grams was a natural hostess. With Emma's housekeeping ability and Rachel's inspired cooking, they should be in good shape.

The cooking was the immediate problem, but surely they could find a way around that until Rachel was well. If Andrea could just get them set up on a sound financial system, the whole thing could work. She might still have doubts about the wisdom of Grams taking on such a project at her age, but at least she was no longer convinced they were headed for disaster.

She pulled up to the garage, giving an approving nod to the lights Cal had installed. It would take a brazen thief to attempt to break in now, even though darkness took over beyond the buildings with only the pale yellow glow from a distant farmhouse to break it.

She parked and walked quickly to the side door that led directly into the family quarters. From upstairs, Barney gave an experimental woof and then quieted, apparently recognizing her step. Grams must have already gone to bed.

Andrea made the rounds of the ground floor, checking the doors that Grams had already no doubt checked. Everything was locked up and secure. She hurried through the library, not looking toward the portrait. Thinking about her grandfather was not conducive to a good night's sleep.

Upstairs, she opened the door to Grams's bedroom. Her grandmother was already asleep, her Bible open on her lap. Barney looked up, tail slapping the floor. Andrea removed the Bible, open to the twenty-third Psalm. Had that comforted Grams enough to send her to sleep? Faint longing moved through her. She wanted…

She wasn't sure what. Faith, like Grams had? Like Cal apparently had? But faith wasn't to be manufactured just because she felt responsibility weighing on her. She turned off the bedside lamp, tiptoed out and shut the door.

A cool breeze wafted into the hall from the open window. She glanced at it, deciding to leave it open, and went on into her bedroom.

The new lights cast reflections on her ceiling. Comforting reflections. They could all sleep well tonight, including Cal. She wouldn't be calling him.

Andrea jolted awake. Shoving the sheet aside, she reached for the bedside lamp, heart pounding. Then the noise came again, and she subsided, relaxing. Thunder, that was all. The threatening storm had arrived. Even as she thought that, rain slashed against the house.

Jumping out of bed, she hurried to the windows, but no sprinkles dampened the wide sills. The rain wasn't coming in this direction, but it might well be raining in the hall window.

She hurried out into the hallway. The sheer white curtains on the window billowed inward, and she rushed to pull down the sash, bare toes curling into a slight dampness on the floor beneath her feet. She could imagine Grams's reaction if she woke to soaked curtains.

There were no lights on this side of the house. Darkness pressed against the panes, mitigated only by reflections of the dim night-light Grams always left on in the hall. She stood there for a moment, looking into the dark, until it was split by a vivid flash of lightning.

She jerked back, gasping. In the brief instant of light—had that been a figure, standing just by the shelter of the lilac hedge?

She pressed her hand against her chest, feeling the thud of her heart. Imagination, that was all. She was spooking herself, seeing menace where there was nothing... But there had been something that night by the toolshed. Was their prowler making another visit?

Lightning snapped again, closer now, one sharp crack illuminating the grounds below as sharply as a spotlight. Showing her the dark figure of a man.

She drew back, clutching the curtain instinctively in front of her, as if he could see her standing there in the flimsy cotton nightshirt. She slid to the side of the window. Stared out, focusing her eyes on the spot, trying to still the rasp of her breath. If the lightning flashed again, she'd be ready.

A volley of lightning, thunder following it so fast that the storm must be right over the house. It showed her, as if in a series of jagged still pictures, the figure turning, the brim of a hat, tilting up toward the window where she stood, frozen. The face was a pale blur, but the clothing—even in dark outline, the clothing looked Amish.

Impossible. But she had to believe the evidence of her own eyes, didn't she? Even as she watched, the figure moved, raising one arm as if he shook his fist at her.

She stumbled backward, heart thudding, breath catching, and then bolted for the bedroom and her cell phone. The doors were locked, he couldn't get in, call Cal, call the police….

Cal answered on the first ring, sounding as if he fought his way awake. "Yes, what?"

"There's someone, a man, out on the east side of the house."

"Andrea?" His voice sharpened. "Are you sure?"

"The lightning makes it as bright as day. He's there, watching the house. We didn't put lights—"

They hadn't thought they needed to where there were no outbuildings to be broken into. Maybe the intruder's goal wasn't the outbuildings. Maybe it was the house itself.

"I'll be right there. Don't go out, you hear me?"

"I won't. I'll go down to the side door and meet you there." She glanced across the hall. "My grandmother's exhausted. I don't want to wake her again unless I have to."

"Right. Don't call the police until I see what's up. And don't open the door." He clicked off without a goodbye.

It wasn't until she stood there shivering in the dark that she realized that at least one part of her relief at hearing his voice on the phone was the conviction that it couldn't be Cal out there in the dark, playing tricks.

Quickly she pulled sweatpants and a sweatshirt on, stuffing her feet into slippers. She hadn't realized she'd been considering that possibility, even subconsciously. But what, as Uncle Nick had said, did they really know about Cal?

Well, she knew now that he wasn't their prowler. And she knew that comfort had flooded through her at the sound of his voice.

Maybe it was better not to dwell on that. She grabbed a flashlight and went softly down the stairs. Should she have called the police? Maybe, but if she did, Grams would waken, would be subjected to that upset yet again.

Wait, as Cal had said. See what he found.

She huddled against the side door, gripping the flashlight, wishing for even the dubious comfort of Barney at this point. If Cal didn't appear soon, she'd have to do something.

A dripping face appeared outside the glass, and her heart threatened to leap from her chest before she recognized Cal. She unlocked the door, trying to ignore the shaking of her fingers, and pulled him in out of the rain.

She switched on the hall light. Like her, Cal wore sweatpants and sweatshirt, but his were wet through.

"I'm sorry. You're soaked." Well, that wasn't very coherent. "Should I call the police?"

"No use." He shook his head, water spraying from his drenched hair. "He's not there now."

"If he ever was?" She knew her quick anger was just reaction to strain. "I saw him. He was there."

"Relax, I believe you. The lilac bushes were broken, the grass tamped down, as if he'd stood there for some time." His fingers closed over hers. They were wet and cold, but somehow they warmed her. "Tell me what you saw."

"A man. I can't say how tall he was—I was looking down from the upstairs window." She kept her voice low, not wanting to stir up the dog. "I didn't make out the face, but Cal—he was wearing Amish clothing."

He frowned. "Are you sure?"

"I know it doesn't make any sense, but I'm sure. Dark pants and jacket, white shirt, the hat—if it wasn't an Amishman, it was someone doing a good imitation."

"I'd almost rather believe that." His voice was troubled. "The Amish aren't exactly noted for producing prowlers. You never met a more law-abiding bunch."

She shivered. "That's not all. It—he—the figure seemed to be looking up at the window where I was standing. He raised his arm, as if he were shaking his fist at me. And if you tell me I was dreaming—"

"I don't doubt you." Without seeming to know he was doing it, Cal pulled her closer. "But we've got to think this through before we do anything. Can you imagine the repercussions if something like this hit the newspapers?"

"I hadn't thought of that, but I see what you mean." Like it or not, and they didn't, the Amish were newsworthy. A story like that could get out of control in hours. She glanced up the stairs. "I don't want Grams upset, and that would devastate her."

"Well, whoever he was, he's gone now." Cal brushed damp hair back from his brow. "Are you okay if we hold off making a decision until we can talk this over in the morning?"

She was insensibly comforted by the way he said *we*. Whatever came, she wasn't alone in this. "Yes, all right. After all, he didn't really do anything except lurk. The house is locked up securely."

"Good." He squeezed her hand. "I'll take another look around before I go back to the barn. We'll talk in the morning. Meantime, try to get some sleep, or your grandmother will want to know why your eyes are so heavy." He turned to go back out into the rain.

"Wait. Do you want an umbrella?"

"Why?" Cal paused on the threshold, his smile flashing. "I can't get any wetter than I already am. Good night. Lock the door."

"No chance I'll forget that."

He vanished almost at once into the darkness beyond

the reach of the light. She locked the door, realizing that she was smiling.

Amazing. If anyone had told her fifteen minutes ago that she'd find anything to smile about tonight, she'd have said they were crazy.

SEVEN

Cal frowned at the mug of coffee in his hand and then set it out of the way on the barn floor. He needed something to get his brain moving after the previous night's alarms, but caffeine wasn't doing the job.

He picked up a sanding block and knelt next to a reproduction of an old-fashioned dry sink, running the fine sandpaper along its grain. This was better than coffee for what ailed him.

What he really needed was to talk with Andrea, but he'd known better than to go to the inn first thing this morning. Katherine would be up and Emma already busy in the kitchen, making it impossible to have a private conversation. He'd have to wait until after their breakfast was over, at least.

He ran his hand along the curved edge of the dry sink's top. Smooth as silk—that was what he wanted. Taking shortcuts at this stage would show up eventually in the finished product, ruining the piece for him.

Even the work didn't chase away his troubled thoughts, unfortunately. He couldn't stop chewing on the implications of what Andrea had seen. Or thought she'd seen.

A few days earlier, he might have been tempted to believe she was making up her tale of a prowler, just to convince her grandmother to sell. Now, he knew her better. Andrea wouldn't do that.

No, he didn't doubt that she'd seen someone, but was it beyond belief that the man, whoever he was, wasn't Amish? She'd seen a figure in dark clothes, but peering out into the storm from an upstairs window, she couldn't have seen all that much. Maybe her imagination had taken the prowler's dark clothing and filled in the rest.

Somehow he didn't relish the idea of bringing that up with her.

"Cal?"

He straightened at the sound of Andrea's voice, dismayed at the flood of pleasure he felt at the sight of her. She stood for a moment in a stripe of sunlight at the barn door.

"Come in. How are you? Nothing else happened, did it?"

She came toward him, the sneakers she wore making little sound on the wide planks of the barn floor. In jeans and a loose denim shirt worn over a white tee, she almost looked as if she belonged here.

"It was quiet enough," she said. "I didn't sleep much, though. I woke at every creak, and believe me, a house that old creaks a lot."

"How about some coffee?" He gestured toward the pot that sat on a rough shelf against the wall. "It won't be as good as Emma's, but at least it's hot."

"None for me, thanks. Grams insisted on giving me three cups of herbal tea this morning, because I looked tired. I don't have room for coffee."

"She didn't ask any difficult questions, I hope." If she'd told her grandmother about what had happened…

Andrea shook her head. "No. And I didn't mention anything about last night." She ran her hand along the top of the dry sink, much as he had done, a wing of silky hair falling across her cheek as she looked down. "But I can't just ignore what happened."

"I know." He frowned, wondering if it were wise, or even possible, to keep her from voicing her suspicions. "Do you want to go to the police?"

"Depends upon what moment you ask me." Her smile flickered. "I spent my wakeful night going over and over it and changing my mind every thirty seconds or so."

He bent, picked up a couple of sanding blocks, and tossed one to her.

She caught it automatically. "What's this for?"

"Try it." He knelt, running his block along the side of the piece. "It's very soothing."

"Just what I need—to be soothed while intruders trample through Grams's yard and try to break in." But she sat down on the floor in front of the dry sink and began sanding lightly.

"Trample?" He raised an eyebrow.

"You know what I mean." She sanded for a moment longer, frowning. "He was there. He was watching the house."

"I know." He silenced the urge to tell her what he thought she should do. It was her decision, not his.

"You're right. This is soothing. How did you learn to do this? The furniture, I mean, not just sanding."

"My dad's father." His voice softened, as it always did at the thought of his grandfather. Whatever he knew about being a good man, as well as a good carpenter, came from him. "He figured everyone should know how to do something useful, just in case."

"He sounds like a wise man."

She glanced up at him, smiling. For an instant their faces were close—so close he could see the flecks of gold in those green eyes, mirroring the gold of her hair. So close he could feel the movement of her breath across his cheek.

Her eyes widened, and he heard the catch of her breath. He put the sanding block down with a hand that wasn't entirely steady and sat back, away from her. That was—well, unexpected. Not surprising that he found her attractive, but shocking in the strength of that pull toward her. And disturbing that she felt it, too.

Andrea looked down at the sandpaper in her hand. She cleared her throat. "Well, I have to make a decision about calling the police."

So they were going to ignore what had just happened. Maybe that was best.

"If you tell the police the person you saw was Amish—"

"I know. It will cause problems, problems for the community, problems for Grams. I don't want that. But I have to do something. I can't help wondering…" She looked at him again, eyes guarded. "What if it was Levi?"

"Levi." He had to adjust his perspective. "That didn't occur to me. Do you have some reason for thinking that?"

She shook her head. "Only that I've seen him around the house. At one time, I'd have said I knew him, but not any longer. Does he ever come over here at night?"

"I've never seen him." Everything in him wanted to reject the idea. "Look, you know he's like a child—a gentle child. If it were Levi last night, he certainly didn't intend any harm. From what I've seen, his parents keep close tabs on him, so it's hard to believe he could have been wandering around after dark."

"Somebody was." She moved restlessly. "You mentioned there'd been some vandalism in the area. Could it have something to do with that?"

"I don't know. The incidents have been pretty harmless, as far as I've heard. Mailboxes knocked down. Somebody threw a bucket of purple paint at an Amish house. The police seem to think it's caused by teenagers looking for a little excitement. Nothing here was damaged, but maybe they're branching out into intimidation." He'd rather imagine it was random mischief, not deliberate malice toward the inn.

She nodded, frowning. "What do you think we should do?"

We. The simple pronoun stopped him for a moment. Andrea considered him an ally. She didn't want to make this decision alone, and she didn't want to worry her elderly grandmother, or Rachel, stuck in a wheelchair. So she'd turned to him.

All the resolutions he'd made about living a detached

life here were on the line. Panic flickered. He couldn't make himself responsible for them.

But he'd put himself in this position. He'd interfered, and he couldn't back away and say it was none of his concern just because his emotions were getting involved.

"It seems to me that the police are already doing about all they can do, under the circumstances. The fact that you saw a prowler again probably wouldn't change anything."

He was being drawn in. He was starting to think like a lawyer again. He didn't want to, but he couldn't help it.

"I suppose not, but doing nothing doesn't resolve the situation."

"Look, why don't you give it a day or two? Let me talk to some of my Amish friends, sound them out about it. See if there's any animosity toward the inn among the Amish community." Doing so might harm the delicate balance of his relationship with them, but the alternative was worse.

She studied him for a moment, as if weighing his sincerity. "All right." She got to her feet too quickly for him to reach out a helping hand. "If you'll do that, I'll talk to Uncle Nick. He may have some ideas, and I'm sure he'd keep anything I tell him in confidence. He wouldn't want to upset Grams."

Obviously Andrea wasn't one to leave everything in someone else's hands, but maybe she was right. Bendick did seem to have his finger in a lot of pies in the township.

"What about Levi? Do you want me to talk to Emma?"

"No. I'll see if I can bring it up without upsetting her." She shook her head. "I'm not looking forward to it."

"Better to talk to her than let the suspicion affect your attitude toward him."

"True enough. If I didn't say it before, thank you, Cal. For last night, and for being willing to help. I appreciate it. And Grams would, if she knew."

"Any time."

He meant it, but he had to be careful. Andrea had broken through barriers he'd thought were completely secure, and trying to deny the attraction he felt was pointless.

But that attraction couldn't go anywhere. The life Andrea prized was the kind of life that had nearly destroyed his soul.

The gold lettering on the plate glass window jolted the cool facade Andrea had meant to maintain for this visit. Unger and Bendick, Real Estate and Insurance. She hadn't imagined that Grandfather's name would still be on the business.

It was a name that stood for something in this quiet country village. Uncle Nick probably hadn't been eager to give that up, and she couldn't blame him.

Grams had assured her that Uncle Nick would be in the office on a Saturday morning. Fortunately she hadn't asked why Andrea wanted to see him.

A bell tinkled when she opened the door. Clever of Uncle Nick to retain the old-fashioned flavor, even when he was dealing with visiting urbanites looking for a little piece of country to call their own. Or maybe especially then.

The woman behind the mission oak desk looked up inquiringly, and in an instant Andrea went from being the appreciative observer to being that ten-year-old trailing her grandfather around town. There was Betty Albertson, her grandfather's faithful secretary, peering at her over the half-glasses she wore at her desk.

Those half-glasses had fascinated Andrea. Betty wore them so far down her pointed nose that they seemed in constant danger of sliding right off, like a sled down Miller's Hill.

"Betty, how nice to see you. It's been a long time." Conventional words, giving her the moment she needed to remind herself that she was no longer ten, no longer interested in the stash of chocolate bars in Betty's top right desk drawer.

Sharp gray eyes now matched gray hair, pulled smoothly back into the same sort of French twist Betty had worn when her hair had been a mousy brown. For a moment she thought the secretary didn't recognize her, but then she smiled.

"Andrea Hampton. Land, it has been a while. You look as if life agrees with you."

Did she? With everything she valued turned upside down in the past few days, it hardly seemed likely.

"I see you're still running Unger and Bendick single-handedly."

The joke had always been that Betty knew more about the business than both partners combined. She'd been so fiercely loyal to Grandfather that it occasionally seemed she resented even the distraction of his family.

Betty's smile tightened. "Mr. Bendick offered to hire more help, but I prefer to handle things on my own."

She'd given offense, even though it hadn't been intended. "I'm sure no one could do it better. My grandfather often said you were worth more than a dozen assistants."

"Did he?" A faint flush warmed Betty's thin cheeks. "That was kind of him. He was always so thoughtful."

Betty had her own memories of Grandfather. "Is Uncle Nick-Mr. Bendick—in? I'd like to see him for a moment."

Betty's gaze flicked toward the closed office door that bore his name, again in faded gold. "This isn't a good time. We get swamped on Saturdays. Why don't I ask him to stop by the house later?"

Andrea glanced around, half amused, half annoyed. "It doesn't look that busy right now. Surely he can spare me a few minutes."

Betty's lips pressed together, nostrils flaring, but then she mustered an unconvincing smile. "He's on the phone. If you want to wait, I'll try to slip you in when he finishes."

Plainly Betty had transferred the devotion she'd once had for Fredrick Unger to his junior partner. "I'll wait." She crossed the faded Oriental carpet to the row of wooden chairs against the far wall and sat.

Betty blinked, perhaps wondering if she'd gone too far. "Well, that's fine. I didn't mean anything, I'm sure."

"I won't take long, I promise."

She couldn't get into an argument with the woman, just because she was hyperprotective of her employer. If anything, she ought to feel sorry for Betty, leading such a narrow life. She probably didn't get out of Churchville from one year to the next. Andrea vaguely remembered an elderly mother that Betty looked after.

The schoolhouse clock on the wall above the desk ticked audibly. As a child, sitting on this same chair, legs swinging, she'd been mesmerized by the jerky movement of the hands. Photos surrounded the clock, recording events from the early days of Churchville. Grandfather at the ground breaking for the school, at the dedication of the bank, at some long-ago Fourth of July celebration.

The door to the inner office opened. Uncle Nick blinked and then hurried toward her, hands out-stretched.

"Andrea, this is a surprise. Betty, why didn't you tell me Andrea was waiting?"

Betty slid the half-glasses down to look over them. "You were on the phone. And now you have an appointment to show the Barker place."

"I certainly have a few minutes to talk with Andrea."

"You know how interested those people are. You don't want to be late."

"Why not? They've kept me waiting at every appointment." He took Andrea's arm, winking at her once his back was turned to Betty. "We have time for a little chat."

He led her into his office and closed the door, then gave her a quick hug. "I'm sorry about that. The woman thinks I can't do a thing unless she reminds me."

"I don't want to mess up a sale."

He shook his head. "Pair of uptight yuppies who think they want a country place but don't like anything that's in their price range." He beamed at her. "I'm glad you stopped in for a visit before you head back to the city."

"As a matter of fact, I'm not going back for a while."

"Now, Andrea, don't tell me you let them talk you into doing something rash. Your job—"

"My job will wait. Right now my family needs me."

His dismayed expression was almost comical. "My dear, I'm sorry. Is your boss all right with your taking time off?"

She shrugged. "He's not happy, but I'm afraid it can't be helped." Her mind flickered to Cal, saying that maybe he'd learn to appreciate her more. "I have to stay, at least until the inn is up and running."

The elderly swivel chair creaked when he sank down in it. His eyes were troubled, and he ran his hand along his jaw.

"I wish we could find some other way of dealing with this."

"I appreciate your concern, Uncle Nick, but it's all right. Really." She took a breath. How to word this without alarming him or sending him running to Grams? "That's actually not what I came to talk to you about."

He blinked. "Is something wrong? Something else, I mean?"

"Not exactly. Well, you know about the prowler. We haven't had any damage, but it made me wonder if there's anyone who might have a grudge against the family."

"Against Katherine?" He sat upright, outrage in his

voice. "Your grandmother is universally respected. You know that."

It was said with such vehemence that she couldn't doubt it was true of him. "Has there been anything— someone who thought Grandfather had treated him unfairly, or some dispute about property lines?"

He was already shaking his head. "Nothing at all. I'm sure the prowler was simply an isolated incident. Those security lights you put up should do the trick."

So he knew about the lights already. She'd forgotten how quickly the township grapevine worked.

"What about turning the house into a bed-and-breakfast? Have there been any ill feelings about that?"

"Mostly from Margaret Allen, maybe a few other old-timers who hate change, don't want to see any more tourists brought in." He shook his head. "They're fighting a losing battle on that one. But I'd say they're not the type to prowl around in the dark, especially Margaret."

He had a point. "She's more likely to bury a person under a pile of platitudes."

"That's our Margaret." He chuckled, then sobered again. "But I'm concerned about you. Your grandmother, dear woman that she is, doesn't understand the sacrifice she's asking you to make. Maybe I could hire someone to help out—"

"Thanks, Uncle Nick." She was touched by his kindness. "I appreciate that, but no."

"Really, my dear." He rose, coming back around the desk. "I want to help. It's the least I can do—"

The door opened and Betty marched in, holding out a briefcase. "Mr. Bendick, you must leave or you'll keep those people waiting." She sounded scandalized at the thought.

"Yes, yes, I'm going." He snatched the case and sent Andrea an apologetic look. "Think about what I said. I'll talk to you later."

She nodded. "I will. Thank you, Uncle Nick."

He hurried out, letting the front door slam behind him.

"He worries about your grandmother," Betty said, her voice almost accusing.

Several annoyed retorts occurred to her, but she suppressed them. "There's no need. I'm there with her, and Cal Burke has been very helpful."

"Well, he would be, wouldn't he?"

Andrea blinked. "What do you mean?"

"It's none of my business, of course." Betty patted the smooth twist of gray hair. "But I'm the one who typed the lease, so I can't help knowing, can I?"

She resisted the impulse to shake the woman. "Knowing what?"

"Why, about his lease on the barn. Mr. Bendick warned your grandmother, but she wouldn't listen."

She took a step toward Betty. "What?" she snapped.

"She's renting that barn to him at a ridiculously low price. Almost nothing. It worried Mr. Bendick something awful. Cal Burke is bound to help out. He doesn't want your grandmother to sell, because then he'd lose the nice deal he talked her into."

The lease clutched in one hand, Andrea charged toward the barn, anger fueling her rush. When she found Cal, he wasn't going to know what hit her. She held on to the anger, knowing at some level that if she let it slip, even more hurtful feelings would surface.

Betrayal. She'd already experienced enough betrayal in her life.

She hurried up the slope and shoved the heavy door aside. Her rush carried her several feet into the barn before she realized she was alone.

She stood for a moment, looking at the scattered pieces of furniture as if Cal might be hiding behind one of them. Nothing split the silence except her own labored breathing.

Instinct sent her outside again, where she looked around, frowning. The inn grounds and the surrounding farmland dozed in the Saturday-afternoon sunshine.

And already the anger was seeping away, leaving space for pain and regret. How could she have been so foolish as to trust the man? She knew better than to let herself be taken in by a plausible stranger, the way Grams undoubtedly had.

Maybe he was in the apartment he'd created for himself in the tack room. She followed the path around the corner of the barn. She'd find him and make him admit that he was taking advantage of her grandmother. If there was an explanation for this...

But there couldn't be. She stifled that notion. There could be no logical reason for Cal to have talked Grams into renting him the barn at what anyone would consider a token amount. No wonder Uncle Nick had been upset.

Upset didn't begin to cover it for her.

She rounded the corner and stopped. She'd been

prepared to find the story-and-a-half tack room annex changed, but she hadn't expected this.

The rough-hewn door had been replaced by a paneled one with nine-pane beveled glass. A bow window curved out at the front of the building, with a flagstone path leading to the entry.

Irritation prickled along her skin. He'd probably talked Grams into paying for all this, creating a cozy nest for himself at someone else's expense.

Her feet flew over the stones, and she gave a peremptory rap on the door.

The door swung open before she had a chance to raise her hand for another knock.

Cal stood there, smiling. Welcoming.

"Good, you're here. How did you make out with Bendick?"

For a moment she could only stare at him. They'd become partners. She'd agreed to investigate with him.

Before she'd known he was a cheat.

She stalked inside. The old tack room had certainly been transformed. Wooden built-ins lined the walls on either side of a fieldstone fireplace. The wide plank floors were dotted with colorful Navajo rugs that contrasted with the solid Pennsylvania Dutch furniture. The open space was living room, dining room, and kitchen combined, with an eating bar separating the kitchen section. An open stairway led up to a loft that must be the bedroom.

Cal closed the door. "Do you like it?"

Anger danced along her nerves. "Yes. Did my grandmother pay for this?"

He blinked. Then his face tightened, brown eyes turning cold. "Maybe you should ask your grandmother that."

"I'm asking you." Small wonder Grams hadn't confided in her about this dubious rental. She'd have known how Andrea would react. If Grams planned to run the inn on these lines, she'd be bankrupt in a month.

Cal looked at her steadily. "You'd better tell me what this is about, Andrea. I'm not good at guessing games."

He leaned against the bar between kitchen and living room, elbows propped on it. The pose might have looked casual, if not for the muscle that twitched in his jaw, belying his outward calm.

"This." She thrust the lease at him, appalled to see that her hand was shaking. "How did you talk my grandmother into this? She might be naive about business, but surely she realized how ridiculous the rent is. And for both your home and your business— you really got a great deal, didn't you?"

He made no move to take the paper, but his hands curled into fists. "Did you talk to your grandmother?"

"I'm talking to you. The person who's cheating her." *The person who lied to me and made me let my guard down. The person I thought I could trust.*

Cal thrust himself away from the counter, taking a step toward her. "You don't believe that." He stopped, shaking his head. "My mistake. I guess you do."

"I was the one who made the mistake. I trusted you." She would not let her voice break. "How could you do this to an old woman?"

His face might have been carved from a block of

wood. "That lease is between your grandmother and me. You don't come into it at all."

"My grandmother asked me to help her with her business."

He raised an eyebrow. "As far as I know, Katherine didn't sign a power of attorney, turning her affairs over to you. If she wants to talk to you about my rental, she will. Are you worried that she's squandering away your inheritance?"

Fury boiled over, threatening to scald anyone in its path. "I'm trying to protect my grandmother from people who would take advantage of her."

Like you, Cal. It wouldn't have been hard to get her to trust you. I did, and I'm a much tougher case than Grams. Something twisted and hurt under the anger.

"I see." Nothing changed in his expression, but he seemed suddenly more distant. "I can't help you, Andrea. The details of my lease are between me and Katherine."

"Anyone who knows the rent you're paying would know you're cheating her."

"That's for Katherine to decide. You're not the owner. And even if you were, you can't throw me out." He nodded toward the paper in her hand. "I have a lease, remember?"

She stared at him, baffled and furious. Then she turned and slammed her way out.

EIGHT

"I don't know what you thought you were doing." The glare Grams directed at Andrea left no doubt about what Grams considered her actions. Interfering.

"I'm trying to help you. That's all." Andrea sat up a bit straighter. Being called onto the library carpet made her feel about eight.

"Going to my tenant behind my back in not helpful, Andrea Katherine."

When Grams resorted to using both names, the situation was serious. "I'm sorry, but I'm worried about you. If you'd let me know how bad the financial situation is—"

"You'd have told me I should sell the place." Grams finished the thought for her. Her face tightened, and she suddenly looked her age. "That's why I didn't tell you. I didn't want to argue about it."

That was more or less what Rachel had said, but how could Andrea keep silent when the people she loved best in the world seemed bent on the wrong course?

"Are you so sure selling wouldn't have been for the best?" She kept her tone soft.

Grams shook her head. "You're more like your grandfather than you want to admit. That's what he would have said, too, even though this place has been in his family for close to two hundred years."

Grams was right about one thing. She didn't care to be told she was like her grandfather.

If saving Unger House meant enough to Grams that she'd go against what she believed Grandfather would have wanted, then no argument of Andrea's would sway her.

"I've already agreed that I'll do all I can to help you. But if you want to involve me in the business, I have to understand what's going on. When Betty told me—"

"Betty!" Grams's nostrils flared. "What right does she have to talk about my concerns, I'd like to know."

"I'm sure she was just reflecting Uncle Nick's feelings." She shouldn't have mentioned Betty. Relations had always been strained between Grandfather's wife and his secretary.

"Nick is a good friend." Grams's face softened. "He worries too much, but he means well."

"I mean well, too, even if you think I'm going about it the wrong way."

"I know that." Grams's voice gentled a little. Maybe the storm was over, even if the problem wasn't resolved. "Rachel and I appreciate the fact that you're willing to stay here and help us."

"I want to get you on a good business basis, so that you have a chance to succeed. As far as the rental is concerned…" She couldn't let it go without trying once more to show Grams that Cal was taking advantage of her. "The barn is yours to do as you like with, but I have to tell you that the rent you're charging is extremely low by current standards."

Grams was already shaking her head. "You don't understand."

"How can I, when you won't tell me about it?"

For a moment the situation hung in the balance. If her grandmother continued to treat her like a child who had to be protected from the facts, this would never work.

Finally Grams nodded. "I suppose you ought to know." She glanced toward the portrait over the fireplace. "When Cal approached me about renting the barn, I couldn't imagine how he'd live there. But he was willing to do all the work on the apartment himself. If you've seen it, you'll have to admit he's done a fine job, and he insisted on paying for everything that went into the renovation."

She'd misjudged him in that respect, at least. To her surprise, Andrea was relieved.

"He's certainly increased the value of the building," she admitted. "But even so, to lock yourself into a contract with that low a rent could be a problem." Cal's turning the lease against her still rankled.

"We agreed that as his business picked up, the rent would increase." Grams flushed, as if she found the discussion of money distasteful. "He insists on paying me more every month, more than he should. I don't want to feel as if I'm accepting charity."

No, Grams wouldn't like that feeling. She had always been the giver, not the recipient.

Andrea took a deep breath. "I'm sorry, Grams. I shouldn't have gone to Cal without talking to you about it first."

"No. You shouldn't have." Grams gave her the look that suggested Andrea's manners weren't up to what was expected of an Unger. "Now I think we'll both see Cal and apologize."

"Both…"

Words failed her. Grams proposed to lead her by the hand and make sure she apologized properly, the way she had when Andrea had left the farm gate open and the Zook cows had gotten out.

"Grams, I can handle this myself. It's my mistake."

Her grandmother stood, every inch the lady. "It was my error, as well, in not telling you. We'll both go."

Apologizing to Cal alone would have been embarrassing. Doing it with Grams looking on was humiliating. It didn't help to know that she deserved it.

If she kept herself busy enough, maybe she could forget that awkward scene with Cal. At least that's what Andrea had been telling herself since Grams left to spend the evening with Rachel at the hospital. Unfortunately, it didn't seem to be working.

She shoved away from the desk in the library, blinking as she tried to focus her eyes on something other than the computer screen. It was getting dark, and she hadn't bothered to turn on any lights.

She stretched, rubbing at the tension in the back of her neck. She'd started entering data for the inn into the desktop hours ago. As far as she could tell, neither

Grams nor Rachel had touched the computer since they'd bought it, supposedly for the business, and that increased her worries over their chances for success. Running a B and B wasn't just about being a good cook or a good host. It was a business. She hadn't been kidding when she'd told Cal about Rachel's idea of a filing system.

And that brought her right back to Cal again. He'd been gracious when she'd apologized. Pleasant, even.

She frowned at Barney, who'd taken up residence on the hearth rug, seeming to transfer his allegiance to her when Grams wasn't around. "I'd be just as happy if he hadn't been so nice about it. You understand, don't you?"

Barney thumped his tail against the rug. The only thing he understood was that someone was talking to him. He rose, stretching very much as she had, and padded over to her. She patted the silky head that pressed against her leg.

"I'm being ridiculous, I suppose."

He didn't comment.

It had been a difficult situation, made worse by Grams accepting part of the responsibility for the misunderstanding. She'd actually admitted that she should have told Andrea the whole story.

That had hit her right in the heart. She didn't want her grandmother to feel any less in charge than she'd always been.

I don't know how to balance all this. The discovery that she was actually taking her problems to God startled her, but it felt right. Maybe Grams's quiet faith was having an impact on her. *Usually I think I can handle anything, but I can't. I need guidance. I have to know what I should do—about Grams, about the inn, even about Cal. Please guide me. Amen.*

Maybe it wasn't the most perfect of prayers, but the admission that she couldn't see her way somehow made her feel a bit better.

And as for Cal having such an inside glimpse of their family dynamics—well, maybe she'd be lucky enough not to be alone with him for the next few days. Or ever.

Barney whined, his head coming up, and he let out a soft woof.

"What is it, boy? Do you hear Grams coming?" She peered out the side window, but there was no sign of a car turning into the drive.

The sheltie whined again, then paced to the door and nosed at it.

"You want to go out? I guess it has been a while." She opened the library door and then followed the dog through to the back hallway.

"Okay, out you go." The lights Cal had installed showed her the garden, the outbuildings, the barn, and beyond them, the dark, silent woods and pasture. All was quiet.

Barney bounded out, the screen door banging behind him. He'd be a few minutes at least, needing to investigate every shadow before coming back inside.

She leaned against the doorjamb, tiredness sinking in. Tomorrow was Sunday, and that meant church with Grams in the morning and an afternoon visit to Rachel. Probably she ought to try and find the rest of the receipts Rachel thought she had saved, just in case any of them required an explanation.

In typical Rachel fashion, the receipts had, her sister thought, been tucked away in one of Grandfather's ledgers, which she vaguely remembered putting on the top shelf of the closet which stored kitchen and dining room linens.

Of course. What a logical place to keep receipts they would need to produce come tax time, to say nothing of Grandfather's ledgers. Rachel hadn't inherited any of his organizational genes, that was clear. Obviously Andrea would either have to do the business taxes for them or hire someone locally who'd keep after them all year long.

She opened the closet, frowning at the creaking that came from the hinges. Sometimes it seemed everything in the house had its own sound, all of them together creating a symphony of creaks, cracks, whines and pops. Hopefully none of their guests would be the nervous sort.

The deep closet had shelves against its back wall, accessible only after she'd moved several metal pails, a corn broom and two mops. What the closet didn't have was a light, but the fixture in the hallway sent enough illumination to show her that there appeared to be a book of some sort on the top shelf, stuck between two roasting pans big enough to cook the largest turkey she could imagine. She'd need something to stand on in order to reach the shelf.

She propped the closet door open with one of the mops and retrieved a chair from the kitchen, glancing out the screen as she passed. No sign of Barney yet. She could only hope he hadn't found a rabbit to chase or worse, a skunk. She doubted they had enough tomato juice in the house to cope with that.

The very fact that she knew the remedy for a dog's encounter with a skunk gave her pause. That certainly wasn't part of her normal urban life. Since she'd been back in this house, all sorts of things were resurfacing from her early years.

Grasping the chair with both hands, she carried it into the closet and climbed onto it. She reached up to find that her fingertips fell inches short of the top shelf. That was what came of having twelve-foot ceilings. How on earth had her sister gotten the book up there to begin with? And why did she think that a logical place to put it?

She could go in search of a stepladder, but maybe if she put her foot on one of the lower shelves, she could boost herself up enough to reach the book.

She wedged her toe between two stacks of table linens that someone, probably Emma, had stored carefully in plastic bags. Bracing her left hand against the wall, she stretched upward, groping with her right. Her fingertips brushed the soft leather cover of the ledger. Memory took her back to Grandfather's desk, sitting on a high stool next to him, watching as he entered figures in a neat row.

This is the proper way to do it, Drea. If I keep the records myself, then I know they're accurate.

She blinked, willing away the childhood memory, and stretched until her hand closed on the edge of the book. Victory in her grasp, she started to pull it down. The palm that was braced against the wall slipped, the chair wobbled, then tipped. In an instant she was falling, tangled helplessly in chair legs and sliding linens, landing with a thud that would probably leave a bruise on her hip.

A board creaked out in the hallway, separate from the clatter of her fall. Before she could look the door slammed shut, leaving her in total darkness.

Her breath caught, and she pressed her lips together. *Don't panic. It's all right. All you have to do is get up and open the door. If you could cope with being trapped in the car and shoved into the toolshed, you can cope with this.*

She untangled herself, willing her heart to stop pounding, and fumbled with sweat-slicked hands for a knob. And realized there was none on the inside of the door.

Be calm. You're all right. Grams will be home soon.

But another voice was drowning out the calm, reasonable adult. It came welling up from someplace deep inside her, erupting with all the violence of a child's terror.

"Let me out!" She pounded on the door, unable to hold back the fear she didn't understand. "Let me out! Someone help me! Help!"

The child inside was crying, hot, helpless tears. *Someone help me. Father, please, help me.*

Cal rounded the corner of the toolshed, his sneakers making little sound on the damp grass. He could see the garage now, illuminated by one of the lights he'd installed, with the door still standing open. Katherine and Andrea must have gone to the hospital to see Rachel.

He frowned absently, coming to a halt and gazing around, probing the shadows, searching for anything that was not as it should be. It would be best if he got back to his own place before they returned. He and Andrea had already butted heads too many times today.

He wasn't sure whether it had been worse to bear her accusations or to listen to her apology. At least when she'd been throwing her fury toward him, he'd had the shield of his righteous anger.

It was only afterward that he began to wonder just how righteous that feeling had been. The hard lessons of the past had driven him to God, but he suspected he still had a lot to learn about living the way God expected.

Andrea had at least been furious with him on behalf of someone else. His feelings had been motivated entirely by something much more personal. He'd thought they'd been on the road to becoming friends. Now it was clear they'd never be that, and disappointment had fueled his anger. Maybe he hadn't expressed it, but he'd felt it, and that was just as bad.

He'd turned to head back to the barn when he saw Barney dash across the garden toward the inn door. Odd. Katherine wouldn't leave the dog outside when the place was empty. How had he gotten out of a locked house?

"Barney!" He took a few steps along the path toward the patio. "What are you doing out here?"

He expected the dog to turn and run to him with his usual exuberant greeting. Instead Barney pawed at the door, ignoring his voice.

The back of his neck prickled. Something wasn't right here. Apprehension pushed him into a trot that covered the rest of the way to the house in seconds.

Even so, by the time he reached Barney, the dog was howling, pawing at the door frantically. Cal grabbed for the collar even as he realized that the noise he heard was more than just the dog.

Somewhere in the house, someone cried for help.

He yanked open the unlocked door, scrambling into the back hall and stumbling over the eager dog. "Barney—"

He shoved the animal out of his way. Barney skidded, claws scrabbling on the bare floor, and then launched his body at the narrow, paneled door of the hall closet.

Dog and door collided with a thud that echoed the pounding from inside. Cal's pulse thudded so loudly in his ears that it took a second to isolate the voice.

Andrea—but an Andrea who was a far cry from the brisk, efficient woman he knew. She sounded terrified. If someone had hurt her...

"It's okay," he shouted. Anything to dispel that panicky note in her voice. "Andrea, it's okay. I'm here. I'll get you out."

"Hurry." Her voice sounded muffled, as if she'd clamped her hand over her mouth.

He grabbed the small knob that released the catch, turned it, and Andrea tumbled into his arms. She grasped him, her fingers digging into his shoulders, her breath coming in harsh gasps.

He'd sensed her claustrophobia when she'd been

closed in the toolshed for seconds. Now—now she was in the grip of a full-blown attack, as terrified as if she'd been faced with death instead of closed-in darkness.

"It's okay." He put his arm around her, feeling the tremors that coursed through her body. "Come with me." He piloted her toward the library, switching on lights as they went, sensing that nothing could be too bright for her at the moment. "You're safe now. Tell me what happened. Did someone hurt you?"

Her hand went up to her mouth as if to hold back sobs. She took one ragged breath and then another, seeming to gain a bit more control with each step they took away from the closet. Barney danced around them, trying to push his way between their legs, making little throaty sounds that sounded sympathetic.

"I'm all right." Andrea probably had to force the words out, and he felt the tension that still gripped her body.

"You're fine," he soothed. He switched on the lamp next to the sofa and eased her to a sitting position. She still gripped his hand tightly, so he sat down next to her.

Barney, balked of his clear intent to take that space, had to be content with putting his head in Andrea's lap.

Cal smoothed his fingers over hers. "Did someone push you? Attack you?" He thought of the dark figure she'd seen out in the rain, and his alarm ratcheted upward. He should search the house, but he couldn't leave her in this state.

"No, nothing like that." She wiped away tears with her fingers. "At least—" She hesitated. "I don't think anyone was there. Probably the door just slammed shut when I lost my balance."

The slight shading of doubt in her voice had all his senses on alert. "Did you see someone? Hear someone?"

"I didn't see anyone."

Andrea straightened, putting up one hand to rub the back of her neck, as if tension had taken up residence there. Her usually precise blond hair tumbled about a face that was paler than usual, and her jeans and white shirt were smudged with dust. None of that was typical of Andrea, but it was somehow endearing.

Focus, he reminded himself. "You didn't see anyone. Did you hear something then?"

She shrugged, attempting a smile that was a mere twitch of her facial muscles. "You know how old houses are. This place makes all sorts of sounds even when it's empty."

"And it makes noises when someone is there. Someone who shouldn't be." His tone was grim. The back door had been standing open. Who knew how many other entrances had been just as accessible?

"I heard a creak that I thought came from the hallway, just before the door swung shut, but that doesn't mean anything. All the floors slant, and the door might swing shut on its own." She sounded as if she were trying to convince herself. "Besides, what could anyone gain by shutting me in a closet?"

Just saying the words put a tremor in her voice. The wave of protectiveness that swept over him startled him with its strength. He had no business feeling that way about Andrea.

He cleared his throat. "Maybe he wanted to keep you

from seeing him. Or maybe—" Another, more disquieting thought hit him. "You're claustrophobic, aren't you? How many people know about that?"

"What do you mean?" Her fingers tightened, digging into his hand, and her voice rose. "Are you saying someone would do that deliberately to upset me?"

"Or to scare you off." He put his other hand over hers in a gesture of comfort and then frowned, groping for a rational thought that seemed to be lost in a sense of awareness of her.

"That's—that's ridiculous." But she didn't sound convinced.

"Look, Andrea, I'm beginning to think there's more going on here than we realize. First Rachel's accident, and then this business with the prowler—either the Hampton women are prey to a lot of bad luck all at once, or someone is willing to go to extremes to keep the inn from opening."

"Rachel." Her eyes darkened with fear as she zeroed in on the possibility of a threat to her sister. "But that was an accident. The police haven't found any evidence of anything else."

"I'm not trying to scare you." He raised a hand to brush a strand of silky hair back from her face. His fingers lingered against the smooth skin of her cheek without his mind forming the intent.

"I'm not afraid." She attempted a smile that trembled on her lips. "In spite of the evidence to the contrary. But Grams, and Rachel—"

"I know. I don't like it, either." He wanted to wipe the worry from her face, but he wouldn't lie to her, pretending everything was all right when it so obviously wasn't. "Maybe I'm wrong. Maybe it's all a coincidence. But I don't like you being alone." Vulnerable, he wanted to add, but suspected she wouldn't appreciate it.

"I'm not alone. You're here. I appreciate—" She looked into his eyes and seemed to lose track of the rest of that sentence.

He understood. His rational thought processes had gone on vacation. All he could think was that she was very close, that her skin warmed to his touch, that he wanted to protect her, comfort her...

He closed the inches that separated them and found her lips. For an instant she held back, and then she leaned into the kiss, hands tightening on his arms, eyes closing. He drew her nearer, trying to deny the emotion that flooded through him, wiping out all his barricades in a rush of feeling.

"Andrea." He murmured her name against her lips, not trusting himself to say more. This shouldn't be happening, but it was. He'd probably regret it later, but now all he wanted was to hold her.

He'd told himself they couldn't be friends. Maybe they couldn't, but maybe they could be much more.

NINE

Andrea wrapped her fingers around the coffee mug, absorbing its heat. The warmth generated by Cal's kiss had dissipated when he'd drawn back, looking as confused by what had happened as she was.

Maybe they'd both sensed the need to change the tempo a bit at that point. Cal had gone to search the house, leaving the dog with her. Barney had padded at her heels while she fixed coffee and carried a tray back to the library, apparently mindful of his duty to guard her. The journal, Rachel's receipts tucked inside, lay next to the computer, the innocent cause of her problems.

She stroked the sheltie's head. In spite of Cal's doubts about Barney's intelligence, the dog had seemed to know she was in trouble.

"Good boy," she told him. "If it hadn't been for you…" Well, she didn't want to think about that.

"If it hadn't been for Barney, you'd still have been all right." Cal came into the room as he spoke. "Your grandmother would have come home and found you soon, even if I hadn't heard the dog."

She knew he was trying to make her feel better, but

she didn't want to think about what she'd have been like if she'd been closed in the closet all this time. Cal didn't understand the panic. No one did who hadn't experienced it.

"Did you find anything wrong anywhere?"

"No actual sign of an intruder, but there are far too many ways into a house this size." He frowned, looking as if he'd like to go around putting bars on the windows. "And I'm not saying that closet door couldn't have swung shut on its own, or even from the vibration when you fell, but it still seems pretty stable."

"Is that supposed to make me sleep well tonight?"

She watched as he took a mug, poured coffee and settled on the couch opposite her. She liked the neat economy of his movements.

"I'd put safety over a good night's sleep anytime." He looked toward the windows. "Your grandmother should be back soon, shouldn't she?"

She glanced at the grandfather clock in the corner and nodded. "I don't want her upset about this. It was just an accident. You agree?"

"Let's say I'm about eighty percent convinced of that. You're sure it wasn't a person you heard before you fell?"

He leaned toward her, propping his elbows on his well-worn jeans. As usual, he wore a flannel shirt, this time over a white tee, the sleeves folded back. Also as usual, his brown hair had fallen forward into his eyes.

"It was a creak. That's all. I told you—this house has a language all its own. Surely if someone had been there, I'd have heard him running away."

An image popped into her mind—the large, dark

figure she'd seen outlined by the lightning. Her fingers tightened on the mug. If he'd been in the house, he would have made more noise than a gentle creak.

"Well, maybe. Unless he was smart enough to slip away the minute he heard you fall."

"You searched the house. You didn't find any signs someone had gotten in," she pointed out.

Lines crinkled around his eyes. "Does that mean you trust me?"

"Yes." The word came out so quickly that the sureness of it startled her. Maybe tomorrow she'd be back to being suspicious of him, but at the moment she was just glad he was here.

"Well…good." He seemed a little taken aback by her quick response. "Have you given any more thought to what I asked you? Does anyone else around here, other than family, know about your claustrophobia?"

She shook her head, wanting to reject the possibility. "I don't know. I suppose someone could. The Zook family probably knew." Levi popped into her mind, and she pushed him out again. He wouldn't remember something like that. "It was a lot worse when I was a child. I don't even remember what triggered it the first time, so I must have been pretty young."

"It didn't start when you left here, then."

She blinked, surprised at his linking the two things. "No. Why would you think that?"

The light from the Tiffany lamp on the end table brought out gold flecks in his eyes. "It's just that I've gathered it was a pretty traumatic time for all of you."

"Has my grandmother talked about our leaving?"

She asked the question carefully, not sure she wanted to hear the answer.

"Only in a general way, saying how much it grieved her when you left."

"It wasn't our choice." Her voice was tart with remembered pain. "The adults in our lives didn't give Rachel and Caro and me any say in what happened."

"They don't, do they? My folks split up when I was twelve, and I always had the feeling that what happened to me was an afterthought. Did your parents—"

She nodded, her throat tight. "Our dad left. Not that he'd been around all that much to begin with." She frowned, trying to look at the past as an adult, not as the child she'd been. "He kept losing jobs, and Mom— well, she couldn't cope. That was why we moved in here, I suppose. Our grandparents were the stable element in our lives."

"And then you lost them, too." Setting his mug aside, he reached across the space between them to take her hands, warming her more than the coffee had.

"My mother quarreled with Grandfather." She shook her head. "I'm not sure what it was all about—maybe about Daddy leaving. It all happened around the same time. I just remember a lot of shouting. And then Mom telling us we were going away, hustling us out of the house before we even had time to pack everything."

"Where did you go?"

She shrugged. "Where *didn't* we go is more like it. Mom never seemed able to settle in one place at a time. We moved constantly, usually one step ahead of the bill collectors."

Her hands were trembling. Silly to be so affected after all this time, but he grasped them tightly in his.

"I'm sorry," he said softly. "I shouldn't have brought it up."

"It's all right. We all grew up okay, in spite of it. And there was a trust fund from my grandparents to see us through college."

"Still, it can't have been easy, having your whole world change so quickly. Is your father a part of your life now?"

"No." Maybe it was odd that his absence didn't bother her more, but he'd never exactly been a hands-on father. "We haven't heard anything from him from that day to this."

"And your mother?"

"She died a couple of years ago. Driving under the influence, apparently. In Las Vegas." She pressed her lips together for a moment. "We hadn't seen much of her since we'd all been out on our own."

He moved his fingers over her hand, offering comfort. "Sounds as if your parents let the three of you down pretty badly."

She shook her head, the words seeming to press against her lips, demanding to be released. "It was Grandfather who let me down. Let us down, I mean. We counted on him. He could have stopped her. But he just stood and watched us leave and never said a word."

All the pain of that betrayal, held at bay over the years she'd been away, came sweeping back, threatening to drown her. That was why she so seldom came here, she knew it now. She didn't want to remember, and the memories were everywhere here.

"You really think your grandfather could have prevented what happened? Unless he was able to have her declared an unfit mother…"

She jerked her hands away. "I don't want to talk about it anymore." He didn't understand. Grandfather—he could do anything, couldn't he? Or was that a ten-year-old's view of the world?

Cal recaptured her hands. "I'm sorry," he said again. He brought her fingers to his lips so that she felt his breath with the words. "I wish I could make it better."

"Thank you." She whispered the words, shaken by the longing she felt to let him comfort her, to close the space between them and be in his arms again…

The sound of car wheels on gravel had her sitting up straight. She drew her hands from his, hoping he couldn't guess what her thoughts had been. She didn't know whether she was glad or sorry that Grams was home, ending this.

"Remember, not a word to Grams. About any of this."

He nodded. Then, too quickly for her to anticipate it, he leaned forward and touched her lips with his.

The organ was still playing behind them when Andrea and her grandmother stepped out into the May sunshine after worship. Andrea tucked her hand unobtrusively into Grams's arm as they went down the two shallow steps to the churchyard. She'd seen the sparkle of tears in Grams's eyes more than once during the service.

Actually, the minister's prayers for Rachel's recovery had made her own eyes damp. She'd expected to feel guilty, if anything, at going back to church after letting regular attendance slip out of her life over the past few years. Instead she'd felt welcomed, and not just by the congregation. The awareness of God's presence, growing in her heart since she'd returned, had intensified to the point that her heart seemed to swell. Grams had looked at her with a question in her eyes once or twice, as if she sensed what was happening.

"I see everyone still gathers out here after the service," she said as they reached the walk and moved away from the steps to allow others to come down. She wasn't ready yet to talk about this renewed sense of God in her life.

People clustered into small groups as they cleared the stairs, exchanging greetings, catching up on the news. A long folding table had been set up to one side, bearing pitchers of iced tea and lemonade. Several children had already started a game of tag among the tilted old gravestones. A few late tulips bloomed, bright red against gray markers.

Grams patted her hand. "Some things don't change. Once you and your sisters did that in your Sunday best."

"I remember. We didn't have any silly superstitions about cemeteries after playing here every Sunday."

The small church, built of the same stone as the inn, was almost completely surrounded by its graveyard, with burials dating back to the early 1700s. A low stone wall enclosed both church and churchyard. Even now, one little girl was emulating a tightrope walker on the top of it.

"Let me guess." Cal spoke from behind her, his low voice sending a pleasurable shiver down her spine. "You used to be the daring young girl walking on the wall."

"Whenever my grandmother wasn't looking." She turned toward him as Grams began talking to the pastor. "I didn't realize you attended church. Here, I mean."

"If you're not House Amish or Mennonite, this is where you worship in Churchville, isn't it?" He glanced toward her grandmother. "Katherine didn't suspect anything last night?" he asked softly.

"She didn't seem to, but it's hard to be sure. When we were kids, we thought she had eyes in the back of her head and an antenna that detected mischief."

"There was probably plenty, with three girls so close in age."

She smiled, shaking her head. "Fights, mostly, over who took what from whom. Caroline, our youngest sister, was such a good actress that she could convince almost anybody of anything. Except Grams, who always seemed to know the truth. I just hope her antenna wasn't working last night."

"She'd probably have said something, if so. She's not one to keep still where people she cares about are concerned."

She nodded, but as her gaze sought her grandmother's erect figure, the smile slipped away. Grams had changed since Grandfather's death, and she hadn't even noticed it. The strength they'd always counted on was still there, but it was muted now. Or maybe Rachel's accident had made her vulnerable.

"I see now how much this place means to her." She pitched her voice low, under the animated chatter that was going on all around them. "I don't want anything that's going on to affect that."

His hand brushed hers in a mute gesture of support. "You can't always protect people, even though you care about them."

She glanced up at him, ready to argue, but maybe he had a point. She'd protected her little sisters during those years under their mother's erratic care, but eventually they'd been on their own. The situation was reversed now with Grams. She'd always been the strong one, and now she had to be protected, preferably without her realization.

Cal raised an eyebrow, lips quirking slightly. "Not going to disagree?"

"I would, but I see one of your favorite people coming. I'm sure you'll want to talk to her."

"Not Margaret." The hunted look in his eyes amused her. "It'll be tough to keep a Sunday state of mind with Margaret spreading her version of good cheer around."

She couldn't respond, because Margaret was swooping down on them. *Swooping* actually seemed the right word—the floating handkerchief sleeves of her print dress fluttered like a butterfly's wings.

"Cal. And Andrea. How nice to see the two of you together. Again. So lovely when young people find each other." Margaret put one hand on Cal's arm, and Andrea suspected it took all of his manners to keep from pulling away.

"We weren't lost," he said shortly. "We were just talking about the inn."

In a way, she supposed they had been, since that was what concerned Grams most at the moment. "Cal's been helping us with some of the repairs," she said. To say nothing of rescuing her from dark closets.

"You are such a sweet boy, to help a neighbor who's in distress."

The expression on Cal's face at being called a sweet boy suggested she'd better intervene before he was reduced to rudeness.

"Just about everyone has been very helpful in getting the inn ready to open." Except Margaret, she supposed. "It's coming together very well."

"Is it?" Shrewdness glinted in Margaret's eyes for an instant. "I was under the impression you're nowhere near ready to open for Memorial Day weekend. Sad, to have to cancel those reservations. It doesn't give the impression of a truly professional establishment. I'd be glad to take those guests, but naturally I'm completely full for that weekend."

"I don't know what makes you think that, but we're not canceling any of our reservations." She certainly hoped that was true. "You'll be pleased to know that we expect to open on schedule."

Margaret's eyes narrowed. "That's delightful. Of course, everyone won't be as happy for you as I am. Still, one has to break eggs to make an omelet." She turned away, sleeves fluttering. "Excuse me. I must go and talk to the dear reverend about the strawberry festival."

Andrea managed to hold back words until the woman was out of earshot. "What did she mean?" she muttered. "Who won't be glad to see us open on time?"

Cal cupped her elbow with his hand. "I think your grandmother's ready to leave."

She planted her feet, frowning at him. "Answer the question, please."

A quick jerk of his hand pulled her close to him, and he lowered his head to speak so no one could hear. "A few of the old-timers don't like the idea of another inn opening, increasing the tourist traffic in town."

"Nick mentioned something about that, but he really made light of their attitude." So light, in fact, that she hadn't considered it since.

"Did he?" He was probably wondering why she hadn't said anything to him. "Well, one of those people has your grandmother cornered at the moment, so I think we'd better go to the rescue."

Grams was talking with Herbert Rush, an old friend of Grandfather's. Or rather, it looked as if he was talking at her—and not about something pleasant, to judge by the color of his face and the way his white eyebrows beetled over snapping blue eyes.

Andrea hurried over, sliding her hand through Grams's arm. "Are you about ready to leave, Grams?" She fought to produce a polite smile. "How are you, Mr. Rush?"

The elderly man transferred his glare to her. "How am I? I'm unhappy, that's how I am. The last thing this village needs is another thing to draw tourists. I wouldn't have believed it of your grandmother. Turning a fine old showplace like Unger House into a tourist trap. Someone should do something about that. Your grandfather must be turning over in his grave."

"On the contrary, I'm sure my grandfather is proud of my grandmother, as he always was." She pinned a smile in place. Grams wouldn't appreciate it if she allowed anger to erupt. She turned toward the gate, grateful for Cal's presence on Grams's other side.

Apparently this place wasn't as idyllic as she'd been thinking, and Grams was getting the full picture of its less appealing side.

He seemed to be making one excuse after another to walk over to the inn these days. Cal rounded the toolshed, checking the outbuildings automatically. Since sunset was still an hour away, he couldn't even tell himself that he was making his nightly rounds.

He wanted to see Andrea again. That was the truth of it. A moment's sensible thought told him that pursuing a relationship with her was a huge mistake, but that didn't seem to be stopping him from finding a reason to be where he might see her.

Well, that wish was going to be disappointed, because a quick glance told him the garage was empty. She and Katherine hadn't returned from their visit to Rachel.

But someone else was around the place, judging by the late-model compact that sat on the verge of the drive. Frowning, he quickened his steps. Probably nothing, but with all the odd things happening lately, it didn't do to take anything for granted.

His muscles tightened. A woman was on the side porch, shading her eyes as she peered through the glass in the door. He shot forward.

"What are you doing?"

He reached the bottom of the steps as she spun around, her mouth forming a silent O of surprise.

"I—you startled me." She grasped the railing. "I'm looking for Andrea Hampton. I knocked, but no one answered."

"She's out just now." The adrenaline ebbed, leaving him feeling he'd been too aggressive. She was younger than he'd thought at first glance, probably no more than twenty-two or three. Blond hair in a stylish, layered cut, a trim suit that looked too dressy for a Sunday afternoon in Churchville, a pair of big brown eyes that fixed on him as if asking for help. "Can I do anything for you?"

She came down the three steps so that they stood facing one another, looking up at him as if he could solve all her problems. "Is she going to be back soon? Ms. Hampton, I mean." Then, seeming to feel something else was called for, she added, "I'm Julie Michaels, her assistant."

He couldn't help the way his eyebrows lifted. So Andrea's office was following her here. "Cal Burke." He wasn't sure what to do with the woman. Telling her to go away certainly wasn't an option, though the urge to do so was strong. "I'm not sure when—"

The sound of tires on gravel took the decision out of his hands. "Here she is now."

At the sight of them, Andrea pulled to a stop in front of the woman's car. She slid out, frowning a little.

He reached Katherine's door and opened it, his gaze on Andrea as she came around the car. "I spotted her looking in the window. Is she really your assistant?"

"She is." There was a note in her voice he couldn't quite define.

Then she walked quickly toward the young woman. "Julie. I'm surprised to see you here."

Surprised and not particularly welcoming, if he read her correctly. Now what was that about? None of his business, of course, but still... He helped Katherine out and closed the door.

"I stopped by to pick up the report."

Andrea's brows lifted. "I said I'd e-mail it in tomorrow. There was no need for you to come all this way."

"I was in the area anyway," she said. "I just thought it would be helpful. I didn't mean to be in the way." Her tone suggested a puppy that had received a swat instead of a pat.

"That was very thoughtful." Katherine stepped forward, holding out her hand. "I'm Andrea's grandmother, Katherine Unger." The glance she shot Andrea said that she was disappointed in her manners.

He was probably the only one who saw Andrea's lips tighten. "I'll get the file for you." She turned and went quickly into the house, leaving the three of them standing awkwardly.

Julie turned toward the patio, her hurt feelings, if that's what it had been, disappearing in a smile. "What a lovely place. You must be a wonderful gardener, Ms. Unger."

"I have a great deal of help. Come onto the patio where you can see the flowers."

He could go back to his workshop, but some instinct made him trail along behind them. Andrea hadn't expected this visit, and she didn't like it. Why?

"I'm sure Andrea must be a big help to you. It's great that she could take time off when you need her." Julie bent to touch the petals of a yellow rose that had just begun to open.

"Yes, yes, it is." Katherine's smile wavered a bit. "I

don't know what I'd do without her at this time, with her sister in the hospital."

"I heard about the accident. I'm so sorry." The woman's words sounded sympathetic, but there was something watchful in those big eyes. "How long do you think you'll need to have Andrea stay?"

That seemed to be his cue. He spoke just as Katherine opened her mouth to respond. "Is that a Japanese beetle on the rosebush?"

Katherine turned away from the woman instantly, bending over to peer anxiously at the small leaves, brushing them with her fingers. "I don't see anything. Are you sure, Cal?"

He guided her a few steps away, keeping her focused on the flowers. "It was over here. I just caught a glimpse."

Knowing Katherine's devotion to her flowers, that should keep her occupied for a few minutes. And off the subject of Andrea's departure. That hadn't been a casual query, and the idea of the woman trying to pump Katherine raised his hackles.

The back door swung open. Andrea strode toward them, a manila folder in her hand. She held it out to Julie.

"Here you are. Please ask Mr. Walker to call me if he has any questions."

"I will." She tucked the folder under her arm. "You have such a lovely home here, Ms. Unger. Thank you for letting me see your garden." She glanced wistfully toward the house.

He took Katherine's arm before she could issue an

invitation to a tour. "Let me give you a hand up the steps. Emma sent one of the grandkids over to mention potato salad and cold ham for a late supper if you came home hungry."

"She spoils me." Katherine took his arm, leaning on it a bit more heavily than usual. "I guess I will go in, now. Goodbye, Ms. Michaels."

He shepherded her into the house and saw her settled in her favorite chair. When he got back outside, the Michaels woman was pulling out of the drive. Andrea sat on the stone wall at the edge of the patio, frowning.

"That wasn't exactly a disinterested call, was it?" He sat down next to her.

She glanced at him, eyebrows lifting. "What do you mean?"

"While you were inside, your assistant tried to pump your grandmother about how long you'd be away from work."

"I should have expected that." Her lips tightened. "Did she succeed?"

"I headed her off. How long has she been trying to look just like you?"

For an instant she stared at him, and then her face relaxed in a slight smile. "You don't miss much. Believe it or not, when I hired her, Julie was just out of college, with brown hair halfway down her back, glasses and a wardrobe that consisted of discount store polyester suits."

"She found a role model in you. I guess that's natural enough."

"At first it was flattering. It took me a while to

realize that she didn't just want to emulate my style of clothing. She wants my job. And she sees my absence from the office as her golden opportunity to step right into my shoes."

"Your boss wouldn't be that stupid, would he?"

She shrugged, eyes worried. "The more days I'm gone, the easier it will be for her. If I stay too long, he may just decide he can do without me altogether." Her fingers clenched on her knees. "I can't let that happen. I can't lose everything I've worked for."

Something twisted inside him. She'd go, just like that. It was what he'd thought all along, but knowing he'd been right about her didn't make him feel any better.

"So that's it. Is your job really more important to you than your family?"

She swung toward him, anger sweeping the anxiety from her face. "I don't think you have the right to ask me that."

Matching anger rose. "Why? Because I'm an interfering outsider?"

"No." Green eyes darkened. "Because you expect me to spill my feelings and share my decisions when you're not willing to tell me a single thing about you."

TEN

She shouldn't have said that. Andrea wanted to refute the words, to deny that she cared in the least about his secrets. But it was already too late. Whatever she did or said now, Cal would know that the imbalance in their relationship mattered to her.

She could feel the tension in him through the inches that separated them, could sense the pressure to shoot to his feet and walk away.

But he didn't. He sat, staring down at the edging stones along the patio, where the setting sun cast wavering shadows from the branches above. His profile was stern, the planes of his face looking as if they'd been carved from one of the planks of wood he used.

Doubt assailed her. Whatever it was that made him look that way—did she really want to know? She sensed that if he told her, that truth could change their relationship in incalculable ways.

He moved slightly, not looking at her—just the slightest shrug, as if he tried to ease the tension from his shoulders.

"You told me once I had too much of a corporate mind-set to be just a carpenter. Remember that?"

"Yes." *I don't want to know.* But she did. She did.

"I was a lawyer." He grimaced slightly. "Guess I still am, in a way, but I'll never practice again."

That was her cue to ask why, but she wasn't ready for that. She settled for an easier question. "Where? Not around here."

"Seattle." He leaned back, bracing his hands on the wall. The pose could have looked relaxed, but it didn't. "You wouldn't know the firm, but it's one of the big guns there."

"Prestigious." Her mind grappled to reconcile the informal country carpenter with a big-city lawyer. Difficult, but she'd always known there was something.

"You could say that. When I landed the position, I knew I had it made. Straight to the big leagues—not bad for an ordinary middle-class kid who didn't even know which fork to use." A thread of bitterness ran through the words. He shot her a sideways glance that questioned. "Can you understand how overwhelming that could be?"

"I think so." Cal had been young, ambitious, intelligent, and he'd gotten the break that ensured his future. She of all people knew what that felt like. "But something went wrong."

His hands clenched against the stone, the knuckles whitening. "Not for a long time. I threw everything into the job, and it paid off. I was on the fast track to partnership, and nothing else mattered."

He was circling the thing that caused him pain,

getting closer and closer. She sensed it, and wanted, like a coward, to close her ears, but she couldn't.

"The senior partner called me in. Assigned me to the case of my career. One of our biggest clients was involved in a child custody dispute with his ex-wife. I was just the sort of aggressive bulldog he wanted to represent him. Win, and opportunities would open to me that I couldn't have imagined."

"You accepted." Of course he had. He wouldn't have evaded that challenge, any more than she would.

"Sure. I threw myself into the case, determined to do the best job any attorney could." He looked at her then, his brown eyes very dark. "I trusted the client. You have to believe that."

She nodded, throat tight. She thought she saw where this was going now, and already his tension infected her, so that her hands pressed tight against the stone, too.

He shrugged, mouth twisting. "I did a great job. Lived up to everyone's expectations. Demolished the opposition and won the case." He was silent for a moment, as if he had to steel himself to say the next thing. "Then I found out that my client had been lying. He really was molesting his six-year-old daughter."

She'd been prepared for it, she'd thought, but it still hit her like a blow to the heart. "The little girl—"

Dear Lord, could anything be worse?

"Yes. The child I gave back to her father."

"It wasn't just you," she said quickly. "It was a judge's decision, surely. And the mother must have had legal representation."

"I told myself that. All the arguments—that it wasn't

just my responsibility, that I had a duty to represent my client, that our legal system is adversarial and everyone deserves representation. It didn't change anything. The bottom line was still the same."

"What did you do?" He'd have done something. She knew that about him.

"Went to the senior partner. He told me to forget it. I'd done my job, and it was out of my hands."

"You couldn't."

"No. Couldn't ignore it. Couldn't go to the mother without putting the whole firm in jeopardy. So I did the only thing open to me. I went to the client and told him either he relinquished custody to his ex-wife, or I blew the whistle on him. It would have meant disbarment or worse, but I'd do it."

He took a deep breath, and she had the sense he hadn't breathed in a long time. She hadn't, either.

"Did it work?"

He nodded. "Guess I was convincing enough, especially when I resigned from the firm." His voice roughened. "I saw the child back into her mother's care, but God alone knows how much damage was done to her in the meantime."

That was the guilt he carried, then. That was why he lived the way he did.

"Cal, you did everything you could. He was the criminal, not you."

He grimaced. "Nice of you to defend me. I spent months trying to tell myself that, until finally God forced me to face the truth. I'd been so ambitious, so determined to succeed, that I'd let myself get sucked into a life that didn't take into account any of the important things, like faith, honesty, other human beings. I had to stop making excuses before I could repent and begin again."

That's what he was doing here, then. Starting over. Looking for peace in this quiet place where values still applied.

"You did the right thing." Maybe her opinion didn't matter, but she had to say it. She met his gaze. "You couldn't have done anything else."

Something in his eyes acknowledged her words. He didn't speak. They didn't touch. But they were closer than if they'd been in each other's arms. She seemed to be aware of everything about him—of every cell in his body, of the blood coursing through his veins.

She took a breath, letting the realization crystallize in her mind. She cared about him, far more than she'd known. She admired him more than she could say.

But what he'd just told her had shut out any possibility of a relationship between them, because the life she longed to keep was the very one he'd never go back to.

Emma, going up the attic steps ahead of Andrea, pushed the door open, letting a shaft of sunlight fall on the rough wooden stairs. Rough, but not dusty, Andrea noticed. Obviously Emma's cleaning fanaticism extended even to the attics of the old house.

"All of the quilts are packed away in trunks," Emma said. "It is good that they'll be useful again."

"I just hope they're still in decent shape after being in storage for so long." She emerged into the attic, which stretched out into the shadowy distance, marked by the looming shapes of discarded furniture.

Lots and lots of furniture. Cal had said the place was packed to the rafters, and he was right. Her unpracticed eye identified a dining room set that surely wasn't genuine Duncan Phyfe, was it?

Emma, weaving her way through odd pieces of furniture, let out an audible sniff. "I put them away proper. They'll just need a bit of airing, that's all."

If Emma had done it, of course it would have been done properly. She was the one who'd suggested the quilts when Andrea and Grams had been debating about drapes and bedcovers for the guest rooms.

"The English will like having Amish-made quilts in the rooms," she'd said matter-of-factly.

She was right. Their guests would come to Lancaster County to see the Amish, who ironically only wanted to be left alone, and they would be thrilled at the idea. So she and Emma were on a hunting expedition in the attic for quilts and anything else that would give the guest rooms a unique touch.

Concentrating on the decorating just might keep her mind from straying back, again and again, to that conversation with Cal the previous day. On second thought, nothing was strong enough to do that.

Cal. He'd wrung her heart with his story, and in the dark silence of the night, she'd found herself filling in all the things he hadn't said.

He'd given up everything—his career, his future, his friends—because it was the right thing to do. Plenty of people would have rationalized away their responsibility in the situation, but not Cal. He'd taken on even more than his share, and now seemed content that it was what God expected of him.

She approached that thought cautiously. Somehow it had never occurred to her, even when she was attending church regularly, that God might have a claim on one's business life. That God might require sacrifice, on occasion. That was an uncomfortable idea, but once planted, it didn't seem amenable to being dismissed.

Emma knelt in front of a carved wooden dower chest, one of several lined up near the window. Andrea hurried to join her, thinking that her jeans were more appropriate to kneeling on the wide-planked floor than Emma's dress.

Concentrate on the task at hand. The practical one was to choose the quilts for the bedrooms. The unspoken one was to use this opportunity to talk to Emma about Levi, to try and get a sense of whether he might have been the dark figure she'd seen the night of the storm.

Leave the theological considerations for later. And any thought of her feelings for Cal for later still.

Emma lifted the chest lid, exposing bundles wrapped in muslin sheets. She took out the first one, unwrapping it. Andrea grasped the sheet and spread it out so that the quilt wouldn't touch the floor.

"Squares in Bars," Emma said, naming the pattern as she unfolded it. "My mother made many quilts for your grandmother. This was one of hers."

Andrea's breath caught as the colors, rich and saturated, glowed like jewels in the sun streaming in the many-paned attic window. The quilt was bordered in a deep forest-green, with the squares done in the blues, maroons, pinks, purples and mauves of Amish clothing.

"It's beautiful." Drawn to touch, she stroked the colors. "Your mother was an artist."

Emma shook her head. "Just usual work. She was quick with the needle, I remember."

That was the closest thing to pride she'd ever heard from Emma.

"Here is one that belongs in your room." Emma pulled back the sheet on the second quilt. "Do you remember?"

Remember? She couldn't speak as the pattern came into view, myriads of diamonds expanding from the center in vivid and unexpected bursts of color. She touched it gently. How many nights had she fallen asleep trying to count the number of diamonds in the quilt?

"I remember," she said softly, her throat going tight. "Your mother made this one, too, didn't she?"

Emma nodded, her plain face softening a little at Andrea's reaction. "Sunshine and Shadow. It was her favorite pattern."

"Is that what it's called? I don't think I ever knew. I can see why—the alternating bands of dark and light are like the bands of sunlight and shadow made by the rails of a fence."

Emma traced a line of dark patches. "It's the pattern of life. Sometimes sun, sometimes shadow. Like Scripture says, 'To everything there is a season, and a time to every purpose under Heaven.' But always God is with us."

The words squeezed her heart. Would Emma consider Levi one of the dark bands? She never seemed to show disappointment or sorrow with him. Maybe this was the moment to ask, but Andrea couldn't seem to force the words out.

"I should put it in a guest room, though, not keep it for myself." But her hands clung to the quilt. Or maybe to the memory of how safe she'd felt, sleeping under it.

Emma shook her head in a decided way. "Your grandmother ordered it from my mother just for you, when she knew you were coming to live here. It made her so happy to fix that room up for you, and how she smiled when it was all finished."

The image came clear in her mind, even from those few words. A younger Emma, a younger Grams, spreading the quilt on her bed, Grams's face lit with pleasure.

"Those were happy times, when we were here," she said, hoping her voice didn't sound as choked as it felt.

"Yes." Emma seemed to be looking back, too. "It was good, all of you children together, those days when the house was so full. We are in the *daadi haus,* now, Eli and Levi and me, and Samuel and his family have the farmhouse."

Andrea sat back on her heels, her arms filled with the quilt. "Does it grieve you, that Levi won't have a family of his own?"

Emma considered for a moment. "No, not grieve. He is as God chose to make him. I accept that as God's will."

The question she had to ask stuck in her throat, and

she pushed it out. "I thought I saw Levi one night from my window. Does he go out after dark by himself?"

"No." The expression on Emma's face couldn't be disguised. Fear. Stark, unreasoning fear filled her face before she bent over the chest, hiding it. "No." Her voice was muffled. "Levi does not go out after nightfall. It would not be right."

Something cold closed around Andrea's heart. The unthinkable had happened. Emma was lying to her.

Cal walked into the hallway of the inn from the kitchen and paused, looking around. He hadn't been in since the painters finished, and he let out a low whistle. Katherine should be pleased. The Three Sisters Inn was a showplace, all right, with the parlors restored to their former grandeur. He might not know much about decorating, but he knew elegant when he saw it.

He put his hand on the newel post, sturdy now since he'd finished the repairs. Emma had said that Andrea needed some help moving things up in the guest rooms. He couldn't very well say no, but he wouldn't mind a little more time elapsing before seeing her again.

He'd told her things he hadn't told anyone else. He'd like to say he didn't know why, but that wouldn't be true. He knew. He cared about her. That was why.

It wouldn't go anywhere, that caring, and she knew that as well as he did. They were too different, and the life she prized was one that he'd never return to.

He started up the stairs. Well, she'd probably be as eager as he was to restore some barriers between them.

He reached the open center hallway on the second

floor and glanced around. The doors stood open to the guest rooms—four on this floor, three more upstairs. Andrea was nowhere to be seen, so he went on up the narrower staircase to the third floor.

The rooms here were smaller and didn't seem quite finished. It looked as if Andrea had been putting most of her efforts into the second floor.

A loud thud sounded somewhere over his head, startling him. He yanked open the door to the attic stairway. "Andrea?" He bolted up the stairs.

"I'm all right." Her voice reassured him as he opened the second door at the top of the stairs.

"Good thing. I thought that was you. What are you trying to do?" He picked his way through pieces of furniture to where she stood.

"I want to take this stand down to the blue bedroom." She tugged at the recalcitrant piece that lay fallen on its side, obviously the thud he'd heard. "It's heavier than it looks."

"It's solid mahogany." He bent to shift it upright, and then took a step back, looking at it. "Nice piece. What's that?" Something had fallen out when the door on the front of the stand swung open.

Andrea picked up several oversize green books. "Grandfather's ledgers." She dusted them off with the tail of her pale blue shirt and flipped one open. "Goodness, this dates back to before I was born."

"Seems like a funny place to store them."

She wrinkled her nose. "Rachel, getting the place ready to turn into an inn. Things that were in her way got stuck into the most unimaginable places. We really should do some serious sorting and organizing. These ledgers should be kept for their part in Unger house history, if nothing else."

She bent over the book. For a moment she was engrossed in her find, and he could watch her as closely as he wanted. With her blond hair pulled back in a ponytail and a streak of dirt on her cheek, she didn't look much like the sleek urban professional.

She glanced up, catching his grin before he could erase it. "What's funny?"

"Just thinking you look a little different, that's all."

"You try rummaging through this attic without getting dirty, in spite of Emma's ferocious cleaning," she said. "You certainly were right about this place. Grams could start selling things off to an antique dealer and fund the inn for the foreseeable future."

"Your grandmother mentioned some interest from one of the local antique dealers, but she's reluctant to part with anything. Or maybe the prospect of sorting seems overwhelming. Are you ready to start an inventory?"

"Don't tempt me." She glanced around as if she'd like to do just that. "You wouldn't believe the stash of handmade quilts Emma and I found up here this morning."

Any potential embarrassment had evaporated in the face of Andrea's calm attitude. She'd found her way back to an easy friendliness, and that was for the best.

"Something you can use, I take it?"

She nodded, but the smile slid from her face. "I had a chance to sound her out about Levi. She insists that he's never out alone at night, so he couldn't be the person I saw."

"Did you believe her?"

She looked at him, distress filling her eyes. "I've known her most of my life. I'd have said she'd never lie. But no, I didn't believe her."

Her voice shook a little on the words, and he knew how much it hurt her.

"I'm sorry. Look, it may not mean anything. If it was Levi, he hasn't come back. Nothing's happened for a couple of days. Whoever he was, our prowler seems to be scared off."

She nodded. "And now that I've mentioned it, I'm sure Emma will make sure that Levi doesn't do any late-night wandering."

"Right." It was worth agreeing to see the concern fade from her eyes. He just hoped they were right and the prowler was a thing of the past.

He seized the stand. "Well, shall we get this downstairs?"

"Yes, thanks. I appreciate the help. Rachel's coming home in a couple of days, and the opening is in less than a week." She tried to take the other side, but he pulled it away from her.

"I've got it. Just do the doors for me."

"Macho," she said, teasing, and went to open the door.

He muscled the stand down the stairs and around the bend at the bottom. Andrea closed the door while he leaned against the wall, trying not to breathe hard.

"Let's leave it here until I have a chance to clean it."

He nodded and started down the next flight of stairs. "Anytime you want heavy moving done, you know who to call."

She followed him. "But—did you want something, before I waylaid you with the stand?"

"Emma sent me upstairs. Guess she thought you could use an extra hand."

"My thanks to both of you." She paused as they approached the landing. "That sounded like the side door." She passed him and hurried on down the stairs.

When they reached the bottom, no one was there. She glanced into the library. "Margaret." She didn't sound especially welcoming. He couldn't say he blamed her.

Margaret scurried across the room, holding out an armload of peonies. "I just brought these in for your sister. I hope you don't mind—I thought they might cheer her long recuperation. Hello, Cal. You're here again, I see."

He nodded. It was probably best to ignore the comment.

"Of course I don't mind." Andrea took the flowers. "But why did you come in the side? Wasn't the front door open?"

"I didn't." Margaret looked surprised. "I came in the front."

He'd have said the sound had been from the side door, too. Odd.

There was a rap at the front door, and James Bendick popped his head in. "Andrea—oh, there you are. And Margaret." He came in, holding a bouquet of pink roses. "I heard Rachel is coming home, so I brought her these, but someone beat me to it. Margaret, those must be straight from your beautiful borders."

Margaret batted her eyes at him. "You're such a flatterer, James."

"This was sweet of you, Uncle Nick." Andrea took the flowers, putting the ledgers down on the drop leaf table in the hallway to do so.

Bendick seemed to be determined to ignore him. Perversely, Cal leaned against the newel post, wondering how long it would take for the man to acknowledge his presence.

"Those look like some of your grandfather's old ledgers." Bendick flipped one open. "Dating back to the Dark Ages, I see."

"Cal and I found them in the attic. I thought Grams might enjoy seeing them."

Having Cal forced on his attention, Bendick nodded. "Burke. Helping out, are you?"

"Just doing the heavy moving." Cal pushed away from the post. "I'll be going, Andrea. Give me a call if you need anything else brought down."

"I will. And thank you, Cal."

If her smile was anything to go by, Andrea must have bought his suggestion that they'd seen the last of their prowler. He just hoped he was right.

He went quickly past the parlors to the side door, reached for it, and then stopped.

The side door was the only one where someone entering wasn't likely to be seen, either from the kitchen or the library. It had been locked when he'd come over. He'd tried it first before entering through the kitchen.

Now the door stood ajar. Someone had come in. Or gone out.

ELEVEN

Andrea sank down in a kitchen chair, grateful for the mug of coffee Emma set in front of her. The morning was only half over, but she'd been working nonstop. It was time to take a break.

Grams sat at the end of the table with her usual cup of tea. "Do you think the bedroom for Rachel is all right? I hate the idea of putting her in the maid's room."

"It's fine," she said quickly, before Grams could get the idea of making a change after all the work they'd already done to prepare a ground floor room for Rachel's homecoming. "She has to be on this floor because of the wheelchair, and that room is perfect. It has its own bath."

"She will be close to the kitchen," Emma added, stirring something in the large yellow mixing bowl. "She will like that, she will."

Obviously Emma was on her side in this. Neither of them wanted to start rearranging furniture at this point.

"Once she's home, we can see if there's anything else we can do to make her more comfortable," Andrea pointed out.

"I suppose you're right." Grams still looked a bit

doubtful, probably over the idea of a daughter of the house being relegated to the maid's room. Rachel had certainly lived in worse when she was in culinary school, but Grams wouldn't want to hear that.

"What are you making, Emma?" A change of subject was in order.

"Rachel's favorite cake. Banana walnut." She emptied a cup of walnuts into the mixture. "Black walnuts from our own tree will make it extra good."

She inhaled the scent of bananas and walnuts. "Smells wonderful. I'd best stay away while it's baking, or I might be tempted to get into it before Rach gets home tomorrow."

Rachel home tomorrow, and the grand opening on the weekend. That would go well—it had to. Of course it would be a shame that Rachel couldn't make her special breakfasts, but Emma would serve hearty Amish meals instead and the guests would be delighted.

And once that was over, she could make plans to get back to work. They would need more help after she left, of course, but Emma's daughter-in-law seemed eager for the work, and she'd pay the salary herself, if necessary.

She glanced at Grams, wondering how she'd feel if Andrea inquired more closely into her finances. She'd opened up a little, but Andrea still didn't feel she had a good handle on how secure Grams was.

And then there was the other regret. Cal. Her mind drifted toward the night they'd kissed, and she pulled it firmly back. There was no sense in thinking about what might have been. They both recognized the attraction and the caring, but the differences between them were just too great.

Still, she couldn't ignore that sense of loss.

"I'm just relieved we've had no further problems with prowlers," Grams said. "I'd hate to have our guests upset. Those lights were a fine idea."

Grams didn't know, of course, about the other incidents, and Andrea had no intention of telling her. There were too many possibilities for troublemakers—Levi, sneak thieves, teenagers intent on vandalism, even the holdouts in the community who were opposed to the decision to open the inn. It didn't really matter who it was, as long as it stopped.

"Andrea?" Grams was looking at her questioningly.

"Yes, I'm sure you're right. There's nothing more to worry about."

Grams reached across the table to touch her hand lightly. "Thanks to you. I don't know what we'd have done without you."

Andrea clasped her grandmother's hand, the fragility of fine bones under the skin making her aware again that Grams needed taking care of. "I loved doing it."

"You have so much business sense." Grams's eyes grew misty. "Just like your grandfather."

She wasn't sure she wanted to be compared to her grandfather, but she knew that to Grams it was a high compliment. "Thank you."

"I'm thinking it's time I turned my business affairs over to you. Nick has been very helpful, of course, but he's not family. You'll do it, won't you?"

For a moment she couldn't speak. If she'd needed

anything to assure her that Grams thought of her as a competent adult, this would do it.

"Of course I will." She blinked back surprising moisture in her eyes. "I'd be honored."

"That is good." Emma used a spatula to get the last bit of batter into the pan and then smoothed the surface with a practiced swirl. "'There is a time to every purpose under Heaven.'" She quoted again the words she'd said earlier, and they seemed to resonate. "A time to turn things over to the younger generation. Eli and me, we still have plenty to do, but now it's our son's turn to manage."

"The Amish know how to do it right," Grams said, smiling. "They build the *daadi haus* for the older couple and turn the farm over to the next generation. Everyone has a role to fill."

"Ja." Emma carried the oblong pan over to the old gas range that took up half of one wall. "It is good to know where you belong."

She bent over, cake pan in one hand, and pulled open the oven door with the other.

There was a loud whooshing sound. Before Andrea could move, flames shot out of the oven, right in Emma's face.

Cal sat beside Andrea on the patio wall, waiting. The paramedics were in the kitchen with Emma. So was her husband, Eli. He and Andrea had been relegated to the outside as unnecessary.

Levi stood next to the gray buggy that was pulled up in the driveway. He'd buried his face in the horse's mane, and once in a while his shoulders shook.

"Do you think I should attempt to comfort him?" Andrea said softly.

He shook his head. "I tried, just before you came out. It seemed to make him worse, so I gave up. He'll be all right as soon as he knows his mother is fine."

"Is she?" Andrea's lips trembled, and she pressed them together in a firm line.

He covered her hand with his where it lay on the stone wall between them, and the irrelevant thought passed through his mind that when she was gone, he wouldn't be able to look at this wall in the same way.

"I'm sure she will be." He hoped he sounded positive.

Her fingers moved slightly under his. "You didn't see. It was awful. Thank goodness Grams knew what to do. She had a wet towel on Emma's face before I'd even figured out what happened."

"I don't suppose you ever saw a gas oven blow out. She probably has. It used to be a fairly common accident, years ago. Since most of the Amish cook with gas, it still happens—did while I was staying out at the Zimmerman place, but luckily no one was hurt."

What about this time? He wasn't sure what he thought, not yet. He didn't want to believe someone had tampered with the stove, but it didn't do to take anything for granted.

"Tell me what happened."

Andrea's face tightened. "I don't want to go over it again."

"I don't suppose you do, but we have to figure out what caused this."

Her eyes met his, startled. "You think it wasn't an accident?"

"I don't know what I think, yet. That's why I want to ask you a few questions." He was surprised to hear that lawyer's voice coming out of his mouth.

She took a breath, seeming to compose herself. "Emma was baking a cake. For Rachel's homecoming. I guess she'd been preheating the oven. Yes, I'm sure she had, because I remember seeing her turn it on." She shrugged. "There isn't anything else to tell. She opened the oven door to put the cake in, and the flames came out in her face." She shivered. "I hate to sound stupid, but what made it do that?"

"The pilot light was blown out—it had to be. The gas built up in the oven, and when the door was opened, that was all it took to ignite."

"It could have happened accidentally." She sounded as if she were trying to convince herself.

"I suppose so," he agreed. "When was the last time the oven was used?"

"Last night—no, I take that back, we didn't use it last night. It would have been in the morning yesterday, when Emma baked."

Something tingled at the back of his mind. "Why did you say last night?"

"Well, it's silly, really. Grams and I were laughing about it. Emma insists on leaving something cooked for our supper, and then I put it in the oven to heat. And she always asks, so I don't even dare to heat it in the microwave. Emma doesn't hold with microwaves."

"It might have been safer, this time."

She nodded. "Anyway, neither of us was very hungry last night, so we just had sandwiches. We were joking about who had to confess to Emma." Her voice shook again, and she turned her hand so that her palm was against his, clasping it tightly. "Cal, it had to be an accident. No one would do that deliberately."

"Maybe. But too many odd things have been happening for me to write them all off as coincidence."

The back door opened. The paramedics came out, carrying their gear, and headed for their truck. Then Eli emerged, supporting Emma, who held a wet dressing to her face. Levi gave an inarticulate cry and shambled toward them.

Eli caught him before he could grasp Emma in a bear hug, talking to him softly and urgently in the low German the Amish used among themselves. Levi nodded, touched his mother's sleeve, and then went to unhitch the horse.

Andrea approached, holding her hand out tentatively. "Emma, I'm so sorry. Are you all right?"

"Ja." Eli answered for her. "The glasses protected her eyes, praise God. Her face is painful, but it will heal."

Emma came from behind the dressing for a moment, her skin red and shiny. "You take care of your grandmother, now. And my cake—"

"Don't start worrying about the cake. You can make another one for Rachel when you're completely recovered."

They watched as Eli and Levi handed her up carefully into the buggy. Levi took the reins.

"I'll come by later to see how you are," Andrea called as the buggy creaked slowly away.

She looked as if she wanted to go after them, do something to make this better. He touched her arm.

"Maybe we'd better check on Katherine."

"Yes, of course." She ran her fingers through her hair. "I'm beginning to think I'm not very good in an emergency."

"You'll do." He followed her into the house, wondering. If this had been deliberate—but there wouldn't be any way to prove it. Still, he wanted a look at the stove.

He got his chance almost immediately, when Andrea, seeing how shaken Katherine was, took her grandmother upstairs to lie down. He waited until they'd disappeared up the steps and then opened the oven door.

When Andrea came back a few minutes later, he was still bending over the open door.

"Did you find anything?"

He shrugged. "Only how easy it would be to blow out the pilot. You'd better have someone come from the gas company to check it out, but I don't think he'll find anything wrong."

He closed the door. Andrea sagged against the kitchen counter, as if her bones had gone limp.

"Rachel comes home tomorrow. The first guests arrive on Saturday, and now Emma is out of action. What could anyone have to gain by tampering with the stove?"

He shrugged. "Someone might have thought it would delay the opening."

"Who would care?" She flung her hands out in frustration.

"Margaret cares. She doesn't want the competition. And there are those who don't want anything to draw more tourists here."

She shook her head at that. "I can't believe anyone would hurt Emma for such a reason."

He hesitated, but she had to know. "It might not have been aimed at Emma."

She blinked. "What do you mean?"

"If anyone knew that you usually heated up supper, the target might have been you."

"But—how would they know? And even if one of us mentioned it, how could they be sure Emma wouldn't take it into her head to bake something?"

He frowned. "That's the thing. Yesterday afternoon, when I came in, I tried the side door, but it was locked. When we came down from the attic, Emma had already gone, but she always uses the back door. I found the side door was not only unlocked, but ajar."

"You mean someone might have come in then and tampered with the stove."

He couldn't tell whether she accepted it or not. "Could have. Could have had a good idea you'd be the next to use it. Could have been a lot of things, but there's no proof."

"No." Her face was pale. "There's not remotely enough to take to the police."

"Maybe I'm being overly suspicious. I hope so. But I don't like it."

"Neither do I." She rubbed her forehead. "It has to be just an accident. There's an innocent explanation for all of this, surely."

"I hope so." He wanted to say he'd protect her, but he didn't know if he could. And he certainly didn't have that right. He reached out to touch her cheek, the caress lingering longer than he intended.

"Take care of yourself, Andrea. Call me if anything, anything at all, strikes you as odd."

"I will."

But she was probably thinking the same thing he was. How did you protect yourself against something as amorphous as this?

"No, thank you, it's wonderful, but I can't eat another bite." Andrea tried to soften the refusal with a smile. Nancy Zook, wife of Eli and Emma's son Samuel, held a cherry pie in one hand and a peach pie in the other. After the huge serving of Schnitz un Knepp—ham hock, dried apples and dumplings—she'd thought she'd never eat again, but Nancy had urged a sliver of pie on her.

"Ah, it's nothing. Soon it will be time to make the strawberry preserves. We will send some over to you." Nancy put the pies down on the table and turned to offer seconds to the rest of the Zook family—Eli, Samuel, their five children and Levi.

Emma was keeping to her bed for the evening, but when Andrea had slipped over to the attached *daadi haus* to see her, she'd been insistent that she'd be back at work soon. Given the painful-looking blisters on her face, Andrea doubted it.

She'd walked over to the Zook farm late in the afternoon to bring get-well wishes and roses from her grandmother. The insistence that she stay to supper had been so strong that she couldn't have refused without insult, especially after they learned that Grams was having supper at the hospital with Rachel.

The room looked much like any farmhouse kitchen, with its wooden cabinets and linoleum floor. A wooden china closet held special dishes. One difference was that the only wall decoration was a large calendar featuring a picture of kittens in a basket. In most Old Order Amish communities, only such a useful picture could be placed on the wall.

She sipped strong coffee, glancing around the long, rectangular table with its covering of checkered oil-cloth. The children chattered amongst themselves softly, mindful of having an English guest. With their round blue eyes and blond hair, the girls in braids, the boys bowl-cut, they looked very alike.

Eli and Samuel talked about the next day's work. Levi sat silent, looking down at his pie. His clean-shaven face was unusual for an Amish adult male, but the beard was a sign of marriage. His soft round cheeks were like those of the children.

Had the figure in the rain had a beard? She wasn't sure. She didn't want to think it, but nothing that had been done would be beyond Levi's capabilities.

She glanced at the gas range. He'd know about the pilot light. But he'd never hurt his mother. That was a ridiculous thought.

A small voice at the back of her mind commented that he might have expected it to be her. All of the Zook family would know about the supper arrangements.

She wanted to reject the idea, but she couldn't. Levi

seemed so uneasy with her presence at the table. He'd sent her only one startled glance when she first sat down, his blue eyes as wide as those of a frightened deer, and since then he'd kept his gaze fixed firmly on his plate, showing her only the top of his blond head.

A low rumble of thunder had all of them looking toward the windows.

"Ach, a storm is coming yet." Eli pushed his chair back. "We must get the outside chores done quickly."

The children scurried from the table, diving toward the door in their eagerness to be first out.

"I'd better leave if I don't want to get soaked on the way home." Andrea rose and held out her hand to Nancy. "Thank you so much for the wonderful meal."

"It's nothing." Nancy bobbed her head in a formal little gesture. "Would you be wanting Levi to walk you back?"

"No." That came too quickly. "I'm sure he has work to do. I'll be fine, but I'd better run."

She hurried out the back door, waving to the children as she headed for the path that went around the pond and through a small woodlot before coming out behind the barn where Cal had his shop.

Thunder rumbled again, closer now. It had been foolish not to bring a jacket, with afternoon thunder-storms forecast. Still, if she hurried, she could probably beat the rain home.

The breeze picked up, ruffling the surface of the pond and making the tall ferns that bordered it sway and dance. The scent of rain was in the air, and lightning flashed along the horizon. The distant farms, each marked by twin silos, seemed to wait for the rain.

She scurried past the pond with a fleeting memory of sailing homemade boats on it with the Zook children. The path plunged between the trees, and it was suddenly dark. She slowed, watching the path, having no desire to trip on a tree root and go sprawling.

A trailing blackberry bramble caught at her slacks, then tugged the laces of her sneakers, pulling one free of its knot. She bent, quickly retying it. Quiet—it was so quiet here. Even the birds must have taken shelter from the coming storm.

But as she rose, a sound froze her in place. Was that a footstep, somewhere behind her?

She looked back, seeing nothing, but the undergrowth was thick enough to hide a figure unless it was close. Too close.

That thought got her feet moving again. Hurry. Don't think about the possibility of someone behind you. Think about the fact that the last thing Cal told you was to be careful. Is this being careful?

Cal. She yanked out her cell phone. Better to risk feeling foolish than get into trouble. She could still feel those strong hands that pushed her into the toolshed.

Cal answered almost at once.

"It's Andrea. I'm on the path coming back from Zook's farm. Maybe I'm being silly, but I thought I heard someone behind me."

"I'm on my way." The connection clicked off.

She'd stopped long enough to make the call, and now the sound was closer. The bushes rustled as if a body forced its way through them.

Could be a deer. But even as she thought the words

she started to run, feet thudding on the path, instinct telling her to flee like a frightened animal.

Around the twists in the path, careful, careful, don't trip. If you fall, he could be on you in a moment.

The sounds behind her were louder now, as if the follower had given up any need for secrecy. She didn't dare look behind her. To lose even a second could allow him to catch up.

Lightning flashed, close now, and the boom of thunder assaulted her ears. She was nearly out of the woods, just a little farther...

She spurted into the open like a cork from a bottle, and as she did the heavens opened. In an instant she was drenched and gasping as if she'd been shoved into a cold shower.

Don't stop, don't stop...

And then she saw Cal running toward her. Relief swept over her. She was safe.

TWELVE

Cal put another small log on the fire he'd started in his fireplace and watched flames shoot up around it. Maybe the fire would warm and comfort Andrea. It was probably better than putting his arms around her, which was his instinctive reaction.

He put the poker back in the rack, glancing toward her. She sat on the sofa, wearing one of his flannel shirts, towel-drying her hair. She looked vulnerable, which made it even harder to keep his distance.

He had to find a way to help her, but he had to do it without wrecking the hard-won peace he'd found since he'd come here. Getting emotionally involved with a woman who couldn't wait to get away from this life would be a mistake. So would reverting to acting and thinking like a lawyer.

"Thanks." Andrea looked up at him, producing a faint smile. "For the fire and the hot chocolate. I've already had enough coffee to keep me up half the night."

He sat down in the armchair, a careful distance from her. "Can you tell me about it now?"

"There's not much to tell." She frowned, absently

toweling the damp hair that clung to her neck. "I'd gone over to see how Emma was, and Nancy insisted I stay for supper. When we noticed the storm coming up, they all scattered to do their chores, and I headed down the path. I'd just reached the woods when I thought I heard someone behind me."

"Back up a little. Did you see where Levi was when you left?"

"I'm not sure. Nancy offered to have him walk me back, but I said no." Her gaze met his. "I'm a little ashamed of that. I'm letting suspicion make a difference in how I treat people. That's not right."

"Maybe so, but it's probably unavoidable. So you don't know where he went at that point?"

"I think he headed for the barn with the boys, but I'm not positive, but just because I was at Zook's farm, that doesn't mean Levi was the one who followed me."

"No, but it's more probable than that someone else was hanging around, watching you."

He could see the shiver that went through her at the suggestion, and regretted it. But somehow they had to get to the bottom of this.

"So you never actually saw the person who followed you."

"No. Just heard him. At first I thought it was an animal, but once I started to run—" She wrapped her arms around her, as if comforting herself, and the too-long sleeves of the shirt flopped over her hands. "I'm sure what I heard was a person."

"I didn't see him, either." He frowned. What could anyone hope to gain by such a stunt?

Andrea shoved her hair back from her face. "That doesn't mean he wasn't there." Her voice was tart.

"I didn't mean that. I'm trying not to think like a lawyer, but old habits die hard." He'd thought he had it licked before Andrea came, involving him in her problems.

That wasn't fair. The trouble had already been here, but something about Andrea's arrival seemed to have brought it out.

"It's not that bad to think like an attorney, is it? After all, you are one."

"I'm a carpenter," he said. "Any resemblance to the person I used to be is a mistake."

A slight frown wrinkled her brows. "I can understand your grief and guilt. But do you think that necessarily means you can't be an attorney?"

His turn to frown. "You think I'm wasting my life here. Is that it? Believe me, I've gained far more than I lost in making the change. Peace. A new relationship with God." He paused, his momentary irritation dissolving. "In my old life, I'd have been embarrassed if someone brought up God in conversation. Am I embarrassing you?"

"No." Her face softened. "Maybe it's the impact of this place. I've thought more about faith since I came back than I had in the past year. Feeling—I don't know. Tugged back, I guess."

"I'm glad." He reached across the space between them to take her hand. Her fingers were cold, and he tried to warm them with his. "Even when you go away…"

He stopped. He didn't want her to leave. That was

the truth, however irrational it might be. She wouldn't stay. Her life was elsewhere.

"When I leave—"

Her eyes met his, and he saw in them exactly what he felt. Longing. Tenderness. Regret.

Be careful. You're not going to kiss her again. It would be a mistake, getting entangled with someone who is determined to leave.

He rose, moving to the fireplace and leaning on the mantel. Take himself out of range.

"As far as this incident is concerned…" He frowned, trying to concentrate on the problem. "Most likely the person who followed you was Levi, simply because no one else could have known you were there. But if stopping the inn from opening is the object of all this harassment, why would he care?"

"I suppose that must be the motive—at least I can't think of any other reasonable hypothesis." She frowned. "It still seems overly dramatic to think that any of these solid, law-abiding Pennsylvania Dutchmen would resort to trying to scare me away just to eliminate another B and B."

"None of it is very logical." He had to get a handle on some aspect of the situation. He might have a better chance of doing that if his heart didn't perform such peculiar acrobatics whenever he looked at Andrea.

"There's still nothing to take to the police. I can just imagine their reaction to my story of being followed coming back from the Zook farm."

"They wouldn't be impressed, I'm afraid." They'd be polite, of course, but what could they do? It wasn't as if she'd been attacked. That thought sent a coldness settling deep inside him. The incident with the stove was an attack, but he couldn't prove it, or that she had been the target.

Andrea glanced at her watch and then shot to her feet. "Look at the time. I have to get home before Grams. I can't let her see me like this."

"You look pretty good to me." He pushed away from the mantel. "Sort of casually disheveled."

"I look as if I've been dragged through a knothole," she said tartly. She started for the door.

He followed her. "I'll walk you back."

"You don't need—"

"I'll walk you back," he repeated firmly, opening the door. "No more wandering around alone, okay?"

He thought she'd flare up at that, but she just nodded. "I'll take the dog with me everywhere I go. He might not be the brightest of creatures, but at least he'll make noise."

He wanted to offer himself instead of the dog, but that wouldn't be wise, not when just being within six feet of her made him want to kiss her. Like now.

He yanked the door open. The rain had subsided to a faint drizzle. "You're right. We'd better go."

Before he gave in to the powerful need to have her in his arms.

"Just grate the cheese." Laughter filled Rachel's voice as she sat in her wheelchair in the kitchen, the table pushed aside to give her more room. "Go on, use the grater. It won't bite you."

"I'm not so sure." Andrea gingerly lifted the metal

grater, wary of its sharp teeth. Still, anything that had Rachel laughing had to be good.

Afternoon sun streamed through the kitchen windows, but she was making a breakfast frittata. At least, she was attempting to. She began grating the cheese into the earthenware bowl Rachel had chosen, trying to keep her fingers out of reach of the grater's teeth.

"You really think I can prepare a breakfast that will satisfy the guests." She frowned. "Make that three breakfasts, if Emma doesn't come back until next week."

"Look at it this way," Rachel said. "You're not so much cooking as being my hands. I'm really cooking. You're following directions."

The cheese stuck on the grater, and she gave it a shove. The bowl tipped, the grater flew up, and cheese sprinkled like snowflakes over the tile floor.

She looked at Rachel. "Your hands just made a mess."

Rachel's lips twitched. Then, as if she couldn't hold it back, she began to laugh.

Andrea glared, but an irrepressible chuckle rose in her throat.

"Go ahead, laugh. I never claimed to be able to cook. That's your department. I eat out or open a frozen dinner, and my cheese comes already grated in a bag."

"I'm sorry." Rachel's green eyes, so like her own, brimmed with laughter. "It's just that you're so competent on the computer and all thumbs in the kitchen."

"It's a good thing there's one area of my life that's under control."

But was it? The computer represented the business world to her, and how could she know what was happening back at the office when she was stuck here? E-mailing her assistant wasn't the same as being there, especially when that assistant had her eyes on Andrea's job.

"I'd be just as out of place in your office," Rachel said. "Here, hand me the bowl. Maybe I can set it in my lap and do the grating."

"No, I'm determined now. I will learn how to do this." She began again, careful to keep the bowl steady. "After all, you'll have to learn how to keep the reservations on the computer after I leave. I'll get to laugh at you then."

"Did you really get all that computerized?" Rachel shook her head. "I kept putting off trying, because it looked so hard."

"It'll be much easier once you get used to it. Much of your traffic will come from the Web site I started, especially when we get some more pictures up. Right now I just have the basics." That was one good thing accomplished, and the computer really would make running the inn easier, if she could get Rachel in the habit of using it.

"I'm astonished. You've done more in two weeks than I did in six months."

She must be getting more sensitive, because she detected immediately the note in Rachel's voice that said she was comparing herself unfavorably with her big sister.

"That's nonsense," she said firmly. "The renovations are all credited to you, and as for the garden…" She glanced out the kitchen window at the borders filled with color. "The guests will love looking at that while they have their breakfast. Always assuming I manage to make anything edible."

"You'll be fine," Rachel said. "You just have to do one main hot dish for each day. We'll serve fresh fruit cups, that special Amish-recipe granola that Grams gets from the farmer's market, and the breads and coffee cakes that Nancy offered to make. It'll be fine."

"Thank goodness for Nancy. She promised us Moravian Sugar Cakes for the first morning. I'll gain a pound just smelling them." She looked down in surprise, realizing she'd actually grated the entire block of cheese without getting any bloody knuckles. "We have to remember to bring flowers in to put on the tables, too."

Rachel nodded, turning the chair so that she could see out the screen door toward the garden. "I wish I'd been able to get the gazebo moved. That was one thing I intended that I didn't get to."

"Move the gazebo?" Andrea glanced out at the white wooden structure with its lacy gingerbread trim. "Why?"

Rachel shook her head. "You really don't have an eye for a garden, do you? It's in quite the wrong place, where it doesn't have a view. It makes the garden look crowded, instead of serving as an accent piece."

"I'll take your word for it." She wiped her hands on a tea towel. "What do I do next?"

Before Rachel could answer, the telephone rang.

Rachel picked it up. "Three Sisters Inn," she said, a note of pride in her voice. But a moment later her face had paled, and she looked at Andrea with panic in her eyes.

"Just a moment, please." She covered the receiver with her hand. "It's Mr. Elliot—has a reservation for the weekend, an anniversary surprise for his wife. He claims he received an e-mail from us, canceling, saying we aren't going to be open yet. You didn't—"

"Of course not." For a moment she stared at her sister, speculations running wildly through her mind. Then she reached for the phone. Redeem the situation first, if she could, and figure out where the blame lay later.

"Mr. Elliot?" It was her businesswoman voice, calm, assured, in control. "I'm terribly sorry about this misunderstanding, but we certainly didn't cancel your reservation."

"You didn't send this e-mail?" He sounded suspicious.

"No, sir, we didn't. My sister has been hospitalized, and perhaps something went out without our knowledge." That made it sound as if they had a vast staff capable of making such an error.

"Seems a sloppy way to run an inn," he muttered, but the anger had gone out of his voice. "So we're still on for the weekend."

"Yes, indeed." She infused her voice with warmth, even as her mind seethed with possibilities. "And we'll provide a very special anniversary cake to surprise your wife. Don't worry about a thing."

When she finally hung up, her hand was shaking.

Rachel stared at her. "They're still coming?"

"Yes. But it's a good thing he was angry enough to want to blow up at us, or we'd never have known."

"The other guests—" Rachel's eyes darkened with concern.

"I'll get the list and call them right away." She hurried into the library, headed for the computer, hearing the wheels of Rachel's chair behind her.

"Maybe we can reach them before they have a chance to make other plans." Rachel sounded as if she were clinging hard to hope.

"Cross your fingers." Andrea paused. "The person who planned this overreached herself. If she'd waited until the last minute, we'd probably have been sitting high and.dry with no guests."

"She?"

"She. I can't prove it, but I know perfectly well who did this."

"It had to be Margaret. She was in the library the other day with access to the computer. She even said something to me Sunday about hearing we wouldn't be able to open in time. But what can I do? There's no way to prove it."

Andrea had spotted Cal making his nightly rounds with a flashlight and called him in. Grams and Rachel had gone to bed early, and the house was quiet.

They sat on the sofa in the old summer kitchen that still bore remnants of the playroom it had been when she and her sisters had lived in the house. Games were stacked on the shelves to the right of the fireplace, and if she opened the closet, she'd find a few toys that Grams hadn't wanted to give away.

Cal frowned, staring absently at the cavernous fireplace. "You could bring a civil suit against her, but that would be using a bazooka to rid the house of mosquitoes."

"Not worthwhile, obviously, but I hate letting her get away with it. And the nerve of her—she just walked in the library when we were upstairs, calmly accessed the reservation records on my computer, and sent the e-mails."

He glanced at her. "The computer was on?"

"Don't remind me of how easy I made it for her. I not only had it on, it was open to the reservations. Well, it's password protected now, but it certainly got us off to a bad start."

"Did you lose any of the reservations?"

"Only one. The others consented to rebook after I'd groveled a bit."

That surprised a smile out of him. "I didn't think you knew how to do that."

"That's a lesson I learned early in my career. If there's a problem, don't waste time defending yourself. Just fix it."

"Not a bad philosophy. I'll bet you didn't know running a B and B would have so much in common with your real life."

His words were a reminder that her time here was coming to an end. She fought to ignore the hollow feeling in the pit of her stomach.

"Anyway, I'm absolutely certain Margaret's guilty of monkeying with the computer, but would she prowl around at night or dress up in Amish clothes to stand out in the rain? I don't think so."

"Anyone with such a fund of insincerity can't be

trusted, but I'm inclined to agree with you about that. She'd be afraid of being caught in an embarrassing position."

"I'd like to catch her at something." She shook her head. "That sounds vengeful, doesn't it? Grams would be ashamed of me. It's just that we've all worked so hard—"

"I know." He squeezed her hand. "Are you ready for guests to arrive on Saturday?"

"I think we're in good shape, but I'm certainly glad Grams didn't tell them they could arrive Friday night. Rachel's been walking me through cooking the breakfast meals. We actually ate my artichoke and sausage frittata for supper, and it wasn't half-bad. And Nancy Zook is providing all the baked goods we need."

He nodded. "I heard from Eli that she's agreed to help out some, at least until Rachel's on her feet again."

"I expect I'll be coming back on weekends, at least through the busy season."

Did that sound as if she were asking for something— some hint of where they stood? She hated having things unresolved.

"I'm glad we'll still get to see you." His tone was as neutral and friendly as if he spoke to Eli Zook.

Maybe that answered the question in her mind. Cal recognized, as she did, that the differences between them were too fundamental. The hole in her midsection seemed to deepen.

Ridiculous. She'd only known him for weeks. But when she looked at him, she realized that wasn't true. Maybe in chronological terms they hadn't known each other long, but she'd met him at a time when her emotions were stretched to the limit and her normal barriers suspended.

And since then she'd relied on him in a way that startled her when she looked at it rationally. Did she have anyone else, even back in Philadelphia, that she would turn to for help as naturally as she'd turned to him?

No. She didn't. And that was a sad commentary on the quality of her life.

Cal apparently wasn't engaging in any deep thoughts over the prospect of her leaving. He was frowning toward the small window in the side wall.

"Shouldn't we be able to see the reflection of the garden lights from here?"

She followed the direction of his gaze, vague unease stirring. "Yes. I'm sure I could see the glow the last time I looked that way."

Cal rose, walking quickly toward the hallway and the back door. She followed. They stopped at the door, peering out at the garden, which was perfectly dark.

"Something's happened to the lights." She couldn't erase the apprehension in her voice.

"It may not be anything major." Cal opened the door, switching on his flashlight. "I connected the new lights to the fuse box in the toolshed. Could have blown a fuse, I guess. I'll go check." He stepped out onto the patio.

"Be careful."

Already at the edge of the patio, he turned to smile at her. "I always am." He lifted the flashlight in a little salute, and then stepped off the flagstones. In an instant he was swallowed up by the dark.

She clutched the door frame, hands cold. Irrational, to be worried over something so simple, but then, plenty of irrational things had been happening. She yanked open the door and stepped outside, driven by some inner compulsion.

The beam of his flashlight was the only clue to Cal's location, halfway to the toolshed. She should have gone with him. She could have held the light while he checked the fuses.

The stillness was shattered by an engine's roar. Lights blazed, slicing through the darkness. She whirled. Something barreled from behind the garage— something that surged across the grass, sound and light paralyzing her.

Cal. Cal was pinned in the powerful twin headlight beams. Before she could move the massive shape rocketed across the garden, straight toward Cal.

Screaming his name, she darted forward. The vehicle cut between them with a deafening roar. She couldn't see—the light from Cal's torch was gone. Where was he?

THIRTEEN

Cal dived away from the oncoming lights, instinct taking over from thought. The roar of the motor deafened him. Something struck his head, and he slammed into the ground.

He couldn't breathe, couldn't think, facedown in the damp grass. He gasped in a gulp of cool air, shaking his head and wincing at the pain.

Think. Look. Try to identify the car.

No, truck—a four-by-four, by the sound of it. He shoved up onto his knees. The vehicle careened through the garden, ripping up flower beds, smashing the birdbath.

He forced his brain to work. It would be gone in an instant. He had to try and identify it. No license plate to be seen—the rear lights were blacked out. He fought the urge to sink back down on the grass, trying to clear his head. It didn't seem to work. Someone was shouting his name.

Andrea. She flew toward him, barreled into him. He winced and would have toppled over but for the hard grasp of her hands.

"You're all right—I thought you were hit." Her fingers clutched at him, and her voice caught on a sob.

He touched his forehead and felt the stickiness of blood, warm on his palm. He leaned on her, aware of the roar of the truck's engine. If he could get a good look at it before it disappeared around the building...

The dark shape had reached the pond. It turned, wheels spinning in the mud left from yesterday's rain. He could make out the shape, not the color. The driver would cut off down the lane....

He didn't. He spun, straightened, and bucketed straight toward them.

He clutched Andrea. Closest shelter, no time—

"Run! The patio—"

Clutching each other, stumbling a little, they ran toward the patio. He forced his feet to slog as if through quicksand, the truck was coming fast, they weren't going to make it, Andrea—

He shoved her with every bit of strength, flinging her toward the stone patio wall. Threw himself forward, the truck so close he felt the breath of the engine. Landed hard again, pain ricocheting through his body.

Metal shrieked as the truck sideswiped the patio wall, scattering stones. He struggled, trying to get to his feet, dazed, left wrist throbbing. Strength knocked out of him. If the truck came back, he was a sitting duck....

Then Andrea grabbed him, pulling him onto the patio, dragging him to safety. The truck made a last defiant pass through the flower beds, charged past the garage, clipping it, and roared off down the dark country road, disappearing into the trees.

Andrea clutched him, her breath coming in ragged gasps. "Are you hurt?"

He shook his head, wincing at the pain. "You…"

It was more important than anything to know that she was safe, but he couldn't seem to form a question.

He tried to focus on her face, white and strained in the circle of light from the door. Katherine stood in the doorway, saying something he couldn't make out, Rachel behind her in the chair.

He had to reassure them. He staggered a step toward them and collapsed onto the flagstones.

"I'm not going to the hospital. I'm fine." Cal might look pale and shaken, but his voice was as firm as always.

Andrea found she could breathe. He'd be all right. That terrible moment when she thought the truck had hit him—she could stop thinking about it now.

But she couldn't kid herself about her feelings for him any longer. That brief instant when she'd thought he was gone had been a lightning flash that seared heart and soul, showing her exactly how much she cared.

The paramedic leaned on the back of a kitchen chair, looking at him doubtfully. "Might be a good idea to let the docs check out that wrist."

"It's a sprain." He cradled his left wrist in his other hand. "The wrap is all I need."

She'd urge him to let them take him to the hospital, but she knew that was futile. She wrapped her fingers around the mug of coffee someone had thrust into her hands, wondering how long it would take for the shaking to stop.

Grams's kitchen was crowded with paramedics and police, but for the first time in her memory, Grams seemed to have given up the reins of hospitality. She sat at the end of the table, robe knotted tightly around her, her face gray and drawn.

Love and fear clutched at Andrea's heart. Grams had to be protected, and she was doing a lousy job of it.

Please, Father, show me what to do. I have to take care of them, and I'm afraid I can't.

The paramedics, apparently giving up on Cal, began packing up their kits, leaving the field to the police.

There were two of them this time. The young patrolman who'd come before stood awkwardly by the door, and the township chief sat at the table. Obviously the authorities took this seriously. As they should. Cal could have been killed.

The chief cleared his throat, gathering their attention. Zachary Burkhalter, he'd introduced himself—tall, lean, with sandy hair and a stolid, strong-boned face. He must be about Cal's age, but he wore an air that said he'd seen it all and nothing could surprise him.

"Maybe you could just go over the whole thing for me, Mr. Burke. Anything you saw or heard might help."

Cal shoved his good hand through his hair, disturbing a tuft of grass that fluttered to the table. She probably had her own share of debris, and she thought longingly of a hot shower.

"I didn't see much. Seemed like it took forever, but it probably wasn't more than a couple of minutes at most. We noticed the outside lights had gone off. I thought it was a fuse, started across toward the toolshed where the box is. The four-by-four was behind the garage, out of sight."

She nodded, agreeing, and the chief's gaze turned to her instantly. Gray eyes, cold as flint.

"You agree with that, Ms. Hampton?"

"Yes. I saw the truck come out from behind the garage. To be exact, I heard it, saw the lights. It crossed the back lawn to the pond, turned around and came back, went past the garage again and down Crossings Road. It took less than five minutes, certainly."

And they'd fought for their lives the whole time.

"Can you identify the driver?" His gaze swiveled back to Cal.

"Too dark without the security lights. As Ms. Hampton said, they'd just gone off."

"That ever happen before?"

"No." Cal's voice was level. "It hadn't."

She knew what he was thinking. Someone could have tampered with the fuse box. Would they have had time to do that and get back to the truck before she and Cal went outside? She wasn't sure, but she couldn't say how long the lights had been off.

"And the truck?" Burkhalter obviously wanted a description they couldn't give.

"The rear lights of the vehicle had been blacked out somehow. It was a four-by-four, some dark color— that's about all I could see." Cal was probably berating himself that he didn't get a better look.

Burkhalter nodded. "We've found it, as a matter of fact."

Cal's brows shot up. "That was fast work, Chief."

"Abandoned down Crossings Road, keys missing, scrapes along the fender from hitting the wall. The back lights had been broken."

"Whose is it?" The question burst out of her mouth. If they knew who was responsible...

Burkhalter's gaze gave nothing away. "Belongs to Bob Duckett. Easy enough for someone to take it—he leaves the garage door standing open and the keys hanging on a hook."

Of course he would. Half the township did that, probably, thinking this place was as safe as it had been fifty years ago.

"Bob Duckett wouldn't do anything like this." Grams finally spoke, her voice thin and reedy.

"No, we're sure he didn't." Burkhalter's tone softened for Grams. Then he looked back at her, and the softness disappeared. "You reported an earlier incident, Ms. Hampton?"

"Yes." She glanced toward the patrolman. "We had a prowler."

"This was considerably uglier than prowling."

She glanced toward Rachel, shaken by the bereft look on her face. Rachel had expended hours of work and loving care on the garden, only to have it devastated in a matter of minutes.

"You have any idea who might want to do this?" He glanced around the table, aiming the question at all of them.

Grams straightened, clasping her hands together. "No one could possibly have anything against us, Chief Burkhalter."

Andrea moved slightly, and Burkhalter was on to it at once. "You don't agree?"

She was conscious of her grandmother's strong will, demanding that she be silent. Well, this once, Grams wouldn't get her way.

"There are people who are opposed to another bed-and-breakfast opening here," she said carefully.

"What people?" Burkhalter wouldn't be content with evasion.

She had to ignore Grams's frown. "Margaret Allen, for one. And I understand Herbert Rush and some of the other old-timers don't like the idea."

"It's ridiculous to think they'd do this."

Grams's tone told her she'd be hearing about this for a while. Grams couldn't imagine anyone she knew stealing a four-by-four to drive it through the grounds, but someone had.

She shivered a little, her gaze meeting Cal's. *Do I say anything about Levi? Surely he couldn't be involved. He doesn't drive, for one thing.*

Cal cradled his left hand, his expression giving nothing away. A bruise was darkening on his forehead. Her heart twisted.

"Could have been teenagers," Burkhalter said. "Hearing their elders talk about the inn, deciding to do something about it. Clever enough, though, for him, or them, to put the vehicle behind the garage while they tampered with the lights. No one would see it there unless they were driving down Crossings Road, and likely enough not even then."

And no one was likely to be going down Crossings

Road at this hour. It led to several Amish farms, but they were probably dark and quiet by this time.

"I trust you're not going to just dismiss this as casual vandalism." Rachel spoke for the first time.

"No, ma'am." Burkhalter's gaze lingered on Rachel for a moment, but Andrea found it impossible to read. "We won't do that." His glance shifted, sweeping around the table. "Anyone have anything else to add?"

Someone stood outside the house one night. Someone might have pushed me into a closet. Someone probably followed me back from the Zook farm yesterday. Someone—Margaret, for choice—tampered with our reservations. There were good reasons for saying none of those things.

"We don't know anything else." Grams's voice had regained some of its command. "Thank you for coming."

Burkhalter rose. "We'll be in touch." He jerked his head to the patrolman, who followed him out the door.

Grams waited until the outer door closed behind them. She stood, pulling her dignity around her like a robe. "Cal, you must stay in the house tonight. Come along, I'll show you to a room. Andrea, please help Rachel back to bed."

She was too tired to argue. Besides, if she did have a chance to speak to Cal privately, what could she say? Her feelings were rubbed too raw to have a hope of hiding them. Maybe it was better this way.

Andrea walked into the breakfast room the next morning, wincing as the bright sunlight hit her face. The

French doors stood open, and Rachel sat in her wheel-chair on the patio.

She walked outside and put her hand on her sister's shoulder in mute sympathy. Rachel reached up to squeeze it.

"Stupid to cry over a garden." Rachel dashed tears away with the back of her hand. "It's just—"

"It was beautiful, and you and Grams made it." Andrea finished the thought, her stomach twisting as she looked at the damage. Dead or dying flowers lay with their roots exposed, and deep ruts cut through the lawn. The birdbath was nothing but scattered pieces, and the patio wall where she and Cal had sat bore a raw, jagged scar where stones had been knocked out. The only thing that hadn't been hit was the gazebo, probably because it stood off to one side.

"It's hard to believe that much damage could be done in a few minutes." Something quivered inside her. It could have been worse, much worse. It could have been Cal or her lying broken on the lawn.

"I am so furious." Rachel pounded her fists against the arms of the wheelchair. "If I could get my hands on the person who did this, I'd show him how it feels to be torn up by the roots."

The fury was so counter to Rachel's personality that Andrea was almost surprised into a laugh. Rachel was a nurturer, yet when something under her care was hurt, she could turn into a mother lion. "Maybe it's a good thing we don't know, then. I'd hate to see my little sister arrested for assault."

"It might be better," Rachel said darkly. "Then I

wouldn't have to see the guests' faces. They'll be here the day after tomorrow, Dree. What are we going to do?" The last words came out almost as a wail.

"We're not going to waste time on anger." She had to give Rachel something to focus on other than the fury that could give way, too easily, to helplessness. "You make a list of what you want, and I'll head out to the nursery first thing. I'll spend the rest of the day putting new plants in. They'll at least last while the guests are here."

Rachel's brows lifted. "You? When was the last time you dug in the dirt?"

"Probably when I left the sandbox stage, but you'll tell me what to do. Look, I know it won't be the same—"

"What about the wall? And the lawn, and the birdbath? It would take an army to get things in shape by Saturday."

Andrea grabbed the chair and turned Rachel to face her. "Look, this is no time to give up. Now stop acting like a baby and go make that list."

"You stop being so bossy." Rachel glared at her for an instant, and then her lips began to quiver. "Um, remind me how old we are again?"

Laughter bubbled up, erasing her annoyance. "About ten and twelve, I think." She gave the chair a shove. "Go on, write the list. We'll make this work. I promise."

Smiling, Rachel wheeled herself through the doorway.

"Rach?"

She turned.

"Has anyone checked on Cal this morning?" She forced the question to sound casual.

"Grams said he was dressed and gone an hour ago," Rachel said. "I'll get some coffee started while I make up the list." At least she looked more herself as she wheeled toward the kitchen.

Andrea walked to the patio wall and surveyed the damage. She might be able to plant flowers, given enough instruction, but this she couldn't fix. Disappointment filtered through her at Cal's absence. She'd expected that today, of all times, he'd be here to help.

Well, he had a business to run. Once that would have been a guaranteed excuse, at least from her perspective. She'd changed, if all she could think was that he should be here.

Stepping over the patio wall, she began to gather the stones that were scattered across the grass. Maybe she couldn't fix the wall, but she could make the area look a little neater.

The stones proved far heavier than she expected. She straightened her back, frowning at one particularly stubborn one.

"Take it easy." Cal's voice spun her around. "I'll do that." The bag he carried in one arm thudded against the wall.

"I thought you left." Did she sound accusing?

"I went to get cement mix to repair the wall." He lifted his eyebrows. "Not very complimentary that you thought I'd desert you this morning."

She wasn't sure what to say to that. "Well, you do have a business to take care of."

"Friends come first," he said shortly.

Are we friends, Cal? What would he say if she

blurted that out? She wasn't sure she even wanted to hear the answer.

Movement beyond him on the lane distracted her. "What on earth…?"

Cal turned. "Looks like the Zook family think friends come first, too."

Her breath caught, and tears welled in her eyes. Three buggies came down the lane, packed with people, and a large farm wagon bore so many flowers that it looked like a float in the homecoming parade.

She could only stand and stare for a moment. And then she bolted toward the house.

"Rachel! Rachel, come here this minute! You're not going to believe this!"

Andrea sat back on her heels, admiring the snapdragons she'd just succeeded in planting with Nancy's help.

"Looks good already." Nancy, Emma's daughter-in-law, smiled, brushing a strand of dark hair back into the neat coil under her prayer cap. "We brought enough flowers, I think."

She nodded. They'd certainly brought enough help. Eli and Cal fitted the last stone into place on the wall, while Nancy's small son stood by holding the bucket with cement. Nancy's husband and another Amish man, their red shirts a bright contrast to black trousers, used a lawn roller to smooth out the ruts. The grass seemed to spring into place in their wake. And the flowers…

"You must have gotten up at dawn to dig all of these plants to bring. We can't thank you enough for this."

"We always get up at dawn," Nancy said. "This is just being neighborly."

All along the flower border figures knelt, setting out new plants to replace the ruined ones. Children ran back and forth, fetching and carrying, the girls with bonnet strings streaming, the boys small replicas of the men.

Funny. When she'd spread the Sunshine and Shadows quilt over her bed this morning, she'd felt that they were locked into a dark stripe. Now the sun had come out. She glanced at Cal, who seemed to be keeping himself busy well away from her. Or maybe it would be more accurate to say that the dark was interwoven with the bright.

A time to plant and a time to pluck up that which is planted.

A clatter of spoon against pan sounded. Emma stood in the doorway. Her face was still red and painful-looking, but she'd arrived with the others and marched into the kitchen. "Breakfast when you are finished. The flowers must be in before the sun is high." She vanished back inside.

The comment seemed to inspire a fresh burst of industry. Nancy handed her another flat of blooms. "Impatiens," she said. "Along where it's shady."

Andrea nodded. The move brought her next to Levi, who was setting out clumps of coralbells. When he saw her, his round blue eyes became even rounder.

"Hi, Levi. Thanks for helping." In the light of day, her suspicions of him seemed silly. Levi was, as he'd always been, an innocent child at heart.

He ducked his head, coloring a little. "Help is good." He seemed to struggle with the words, and she realized he'd be far more comfortable with the language of the home. Unfortunately, she'd forgotten whatever German she'd learned as a child.

"Yes. You're good neighbors."

He stared at her, and she saw to her horror that his eyes were filling with tears. "Sorry. Sorry."

He scrambled to his feet, arms flailing awkwardly, and ran toward the barn.

She was still staring after him when Nancy knelt next to her, picking up the trowel he'd dropped and finishing the planting in a few deft movements. "It makes no trouble. Levi will be fine. One of the children will get him when it's time to eat."

"I didn't mean to upset him."

"He's been—" she paused, seeming to search for a word "—funny, just lately. He'll be all right."

"You don't know what's causing it?"

Nancy shrugged. "He doesn't talk so much. Sooner or later he will tell his mother, and she will make it right. Some simple thing, most likely."

Nancy was probably right. She certainly knew Levi better than Andrea did.

Still, she couldn't help but wonder. Why had Levi begun to cry at the sight of her? And why had he said he was sorry?

FOURTEEN

Cal pulled into the driveway and stopped close to the back garden. He'd seen Rachel mourning over the pieces of the birdbath earlier. The one he'd found at the garden store out toward Lancaster should be a decent replacement.

He got the wheelbarrow from the utility shed in the garage, struggling to manage it. Even with his wrist taped, using that hand was awkward. Lucky it wasn't the right, or he'd be out of work until it healed.

Andrea emerged onto the patio, carrying a watering can. She checked at the sight of him, then waved and began sprinkling the potted plants along the edge of the patio.

Maybe Andrea hadn't quite figured out what had changed between them last night, either. He hefted the birdbath onto the wheelbarrow with one hand. They were both trying to look busy, which probably meant they were both confused.

During those moments when they'd fought for their lives, there hadn't been time to think, only to act and feel. Trouble was, he felt too much.

*Lord, does it make any sense at all for me to fall for
someone like Andrea? If You've taught me anything in
the past year, isn't it that this is the life that's right for
me? Andrea could never be content with that. She's
itching to race back to the city the minute she's free.*

If he told her what he felt—but that could only lead
to pain and awkwardness between them.

He was maneuvering the birdbath into place when
Andrea caught the opposite side and helped him.

"This is lovely. Where did you find it?"

"Little place over toward Lancaster." If he looked at
her, he might weaken, so it was better to concentrate
on getting the birdbath into exactly the right spot. "I
thought it would please Rachel."

"She'll be delighted." Her tone had cooled in response to his.

He hated that. But wasn't it better for both of them
in the long run? Why start something that could only
end badly?

Andrea touched a scalloped edge. "About last
night…"

He tensed, but before she could say anything else, a
buggy came down the drive, the horse driven at a fast
trot. "It's Eli." He went to meet the buggy, aware of
Andrea hurrying beside him.

Eli pulled up. "Have you seen our Levi since this
morning?"

"No, not since we were working on the lawn." He
glanced at Andrea, and she shook her head. "Is something wrong?"

"No one has seen him all day." The lines of his face

deepened. "That's not like him. He never goes far, and he always tells his mother. We are starting a search."

Cal glanced at his watch. Nearly five. Levi had been missing for something like seven hours.

"What can we do to help?" Andrea said.

"Search all your buildings. And pray."

"We'll do both," he said quickly. "If we spot him, we'll ring the bell." He nodded toward the old-fashioned dinner bell that hung next to the kitchen door.

"I must tell the other neighbors." Eli was already turning the buggy, and he rolled off without another word. The Amish habit of leaving off the niceties of conversation could seem abrupt, but it was certainly understandable now.

Andrea glanced toward the house. "Grams and Rachel are resting, and they wouldn't be much help in any event."

He headed for the garage. "They don't need to know yet. We can start at this end and work our way out toward the barn."

While he checked the cars and the garage loft, Andrea opened the door to the attached utility shed.

By the time he came back down, she was dusting her hands off. "Nothing in there but a lot of spiderwebs." She hesitated a moment, as if something was on her mind. "You know, Levi was a little odd this morning."

"Odd in what way?" He headed for the old brooder coop, which stood next in the line of outbuildings.

"He was upset when he realized I was working next to him." She seemed to be choosing her words carefully. "I tried to talk to him, but all he'd say was that he was sorry. Then he ran off, almost in tears."

"You didn't get a sense of what it was all about?"

She shook her head. "When I mentioned it to Nancy, she said he'd been withdrawn lately, but she didn't take it seriously."

"What could he have been sorry for? For what happened last night?"

"I don't know." She brushed her hair free of the collar of her shirt with an irritated movement. "Does that seem very likely? He doesn't know how to drive, does he?"

He flung open the door of the brooder coop. It was packed solidly with furniture. "A mouse couldn't hide in here." He closed the door again. "I wouldn't think Levi could drive, but a surprising number of Amish people can. Learn when they are teens, most of them. What direction did Levi head when he ran off?"

"Toward the barn—yours, not the old one. But wouldn't you have seen him if he were there?"

"I haven't been in all day. Too much else to do. Maybe we'd better check there next."

She nodded, trotting beside him as he quickened his pace. It wasn't the first time Levi had wandered off, but he didn't generally go farther than the Unger place. Levi could have decided to take refuge in the barn, he supposed, hiding from some imagined misdeed.

They hurried up the earthen ramp, and he pulled the door open.

"Levi! Levi, are you in here?" The words echoed in the barn's lofty spaces.

Andrea grabbed his arm. "The trapdoor to the lower level. It's open."

He swung around, following the direction of her pointing finger. The hatch, used long ago to throw hay down to the stalls in the lower level, was always kept closed and bolted. Now it yawned open.

He was there in an instant, bending to peer down into the shadowy depths. His heart jolted into overtime.

Levi lay on the floor below, arms outstretched, blood darkening the straw beneath his head. His hands were open, palm up, and next to his right hand, glinting in the shaft of sunlight that pierced the dimness, lay a ring of car keys.

Andrea sat on the plastic chair in the hospital waiting room. She glanced at her watch. How much longer? Surely the doctors knew something by now. At least they'd been given this secluded room in which to wait, rather than sitting out in the open where others could stare at the quaintly dressed Amish.

Grams sat bolt upright on her chair, as if to show any sign of weakness would be a betrayal. She had her arm around Emma, who wept softly into a handkerchief. Nancy sat on Emma's other side, having left the children with Rachel, who'd been quick to say she'd be more trouble than she was worth at the hospital.

Men clustered in a group in the far corner, drinking coffee and talking in low voices. Every now and then the door opened and more Amish appeared, quickly segregating themselves by sexes. A carryover from their separation in church or simply a male desire to be as far away as possible from female tears.

The men's black jackets, the women's black bonnets

seemed almost a sign of mourning. She shook off that thought. Levi would be all right. He'd been breathing on his own when they brought him in. That was a good sign, wasn't it?

Each time the door opened, all eyes went to it. Each time, Emma sobbed a bit more.

"I don't understand." Emma's wail was loud enough to startle even the men. "Why did Levi go to the barn? How did he fall?"

Grams took the twisting hands in hers. "We'll know when he's well enough to tell you," she said firmly.

Eli came to his wife and patted her awkwardly on the shoulder. "We must accept," he said. "It is God's will."

Was it? The questions that had hovered at the back of Andrea's mind since she and Cal found Levi forced their way to the front. Her eyes sought out Cal. He was filling his foam cup at the coffee urn, but, as if he felt her gaze on him, he looked up and brought the cup to her.

"Have some. I know it's awful, but at least it's hot."

She took the cup, rising and moving toward the window, where they had the illusion of privacy. "Do you really believe Levi could have driven that truck?" She kept her voice low.

He glanced toward the group around Eli before answering. "It's starting to look that way. Samuel admits that Levi was fascinated by cars. He thinks some of the local teenagers might have thought it was funny to show him." He shook his head. "I just can't figure out how he'd get away from home last night. Emma has been keeping pretty close tabs on him."

"She has, but she was probably exhausted. I don't see how he'd have gotten the keys if he didn't do it. Unless the driver dropped them someplace and he picked them up. And assuming they're the keys to the truck."

"Maybe we're going to find out."

The door had swung open again. This time it was Chief Burkhalter. He glanced around the room, seeming surprised to find it so crowded.

"Any word yet on the boy's condition?" He directed the question to Eli.

Eli shook his head. His normally ruddy face was gray with pain. "The doctor will come when they've finished," he said.

"In that case..." His gaze singled out the two of them. "Maybe you'd step outside so we can have a word, since you found him."

She was grateful for Cal's hand on her back as they followed Burkhalter out into the hallway, knowing everyone watched them go. In the corridor, he gestured them into a room a few doors away.

It was a replica of the other waiting room with its pale green walls and generic landscapes. The chairs looked just as uncomfortable. Burkhalter jerked three of them into a circle. At his commanding look, they sat.

She had nothing to feel guilty about, did she? So why did she feel as if she wanted to look anywhere except into Burkhalter's face?

"Tell me about finding him."

Cal nodded. "Eli came over to tell us he was missing and asked us to search the property. Ms. Hampton and

I happened to be out in the garden at the time. We started searching the outbuildings."

"It didn't occur to you to look in the inn first?"

Andrea blinked. "I suppose I knew it was unlikely Levi would go inside. He's—well, skittish around strangers." She thought of the rabbits that looked askance when she came out onto the lawn and hopped quickly away.

"So you started searching. What took you to the barn?"

"I remembered that he had gone that way when he left the group that was repairing the damage from last night." She closed her mouth, reluctant to say anything that might contribute to his suspicion.

"Did you talk to him at all this morning?" The man seemed to have radar for evasions.

"Yes, a little. He seemed upset." She darted a glance toward Cal, but he couldn't help her. "He said he was sorry."

"Sorry about what?" Burkhalter's response was like the crack of a whip.

"He didn't say. He ran off." She shook her head to forestall any questions. "There's no point in asking me anything else. That's all I know. I remembered he went toward the barn, so we went there. We saw the trapdoor open." Her voice shook a little, and Cal's hand closed hard over hers. "We found him."

Burkhalter transferred his gaze to Cal. "That trapdoor. You always leave it open?"

"No. I always keep it closed and bolted."

"What did you do after you spotted him?"

"Called paramedics. Went down to see if we could

help him." Cal had apparently decided he could be as laconic as Burkhalter.

"I ran back to the house to ring the dinner bell," she said. "We'd agreed that's what we'd do if we found him."

Burkhalter nodded, his gaze fixed on her face. "You know, Ms. Hampton, whenever the police get called in, people get choosy about what they say. Mostly it's innocent enough, but they don't want to say more than they have to. Wouldn't you agree, Counselor?"

If Cal was surprised that the chief knew about his past, he didn't betray it. "Maybe so, if they think it's unimportant."

"Cops get so they have a sense when someone's hiding something." He turned on Andrea. "How about it, Ms. Hampton? What aren't you telling me?"

She blinked. He really did have radar. "It's nothing."

"Tell me anyway, and let me decide if it's nothing."

She brushed the hair back from her face. She had no choice, and surely nothing she said could make matters any worse now.

"There was another incident, after the prowler call. I was locked in the downstairs pantry. I thought it was an accident—maybe I bumped the door myself."

"And what else?"

"One night when it was storming, I went to close the windows. I saw someone standing out on the lawn, watching the house." She hesitated. "It appeared to be a man in Amish clothing. I couldn't identify him any further."

"She called me," Cal said. "I came over—didn't catch him, but I found the place where he'd been standing. Judging by the way the grass was trampled, he'd been there for quite a while."

Burkhalter made a show of consulting a small notebook. "I understand your housekeeper had an accident with the stove."

"Yes." Levi wouldn't do anything to hurt his own mother. Surely Burkhalter could see that. "The repairman couldn't say whether someone had tampered with it or not. It could have been an accident."

"Quite a string of bad luck you folks have been having," he observed.

She waited for him to probe more deeply, but to her surprise, he rose.

"You can join the others, if you like."

"Chief." Cal's voice stopped him at the doorway. "Those keys—were they the keys to the stolen truck?"

He didn't move for a moment. Would he answer?

"Yes," he said. "They were."

The stack of green ledgers in the middle of the library desk gave Andrea pause. Rachel, searching in the lower kitchen cabinets for a bundt cake pan, had unearthed yet another batch of Grandfather's records that she'd put away in an unlikely place. Andrea had delivered a lecture on organization, but doubted whether it would do any good.

Andrea pushed the ledgers to one side and switched on the computer, feeling too tired to deal with much of anything this morning. The doctors had come out at last and announced that Levi had a severe concussion and several broken ribs, but would mend. Emma's tears had turned to rejoicing, and the bishop, a local farmer named Christian Lapp, led a lengthy prayer of thanksgiving.

Finally she'd persuaded Grams to come home. It had been nearly one before the house was quiet, and then she'd lain awake, unable to turn off the questions in her mind.

They'd all come down to one, in the end. Why? Why would Levi do such a thing? Until he told them, no one would know.

Guests were arriving tomorrow. She shoved her hair back and called up the reservations on the computer screen. Were they ready? Aside from a sense that all of them would have difficulty playing the genial host, she thought so.

The front door opened. "Hello?"

"In the library." She shoved her chair back, but the visitor came in even as she rose.

Betty. For a moment it seemed odd, seeing the woman anywhere but behind her desk at Unger and Bendick.

"Betty." She gave what she hoped was a welcoming smile. "What brings you to see us?"

There was no returning smile. Betty marched to the desk and set down a stack of file folders and several computer disks. "Mr. Bendick asked me to bring these to you."

Andrea stared at them blankly. "I'm sorry?"

Betty's lips pressed together in an offended line. "Mrs. Unger informed him that you would be handling all her finances in the future."

With everything else that had been happening, she'd forgotten that vote of confidence from Grams. "I see. I didn't intend for you to bring those over. I'd have come in to talk with Uncle Nick."

"He thought this would be best." Even Betty's hair, piled in some sort of complicated knot on her head, seemed to quiver with indignation.

It looked as if she'd have to mend some fences. "My grandmother didn't intend any lack of confidence in Uncle Nick. She appreciates everything he's done, but she thought she'd have me do it rather than to take advantage of him, as busy as he is."

Betty leaned over to flip open the top folder. "There are forms here that Mrs. Unger must sign. Please have her do so."

Obviously Betty was offended on Nick's behalf. She found it hard to believe that Nick cared all that much. Surely managing Grams's affairs was an extra burden he didn't need.

"I'll have her sign them when she gets back from the hospital."

Betty paused, and Andrea could see her need to hold on to the grudge battling her curiosity. The curiosity won.

"Is she visiting that Zook boy who caused all the trouble?" Incredulity filled her voice.

"My grandmother is good friends with the Zook family." Andrea stood. "Thank you for dropping these off. I'll take care of them."

Betty glared at her for a moment. Then she turned and stalked out. The front door slammed.

"She isn't too happy with you." Cal walked in from the kitchen as she sat down.

She felt the little jolt to her heart that seemed to

come with his presence. "Did you bring my grandmother back from the hospital?"

"She wanted to stay a while longer, so Emma ar-
ranged for someone to pick them both up. I told Katherine I'd stop by and update you."

"How is Levi?"

He came and perched on the corner of the desk.
"The doctors seem satisfied. He should come home in
a few days, if all continues to go well."

That was good news, but where did they go from
there? "Has he said anything? Explained?"

He shook his head. "He's conscious, but he doesn't
seem to remember much about his injury. Burkhalter
tried to question him, but Levi got so upset he gave up."
He shrugged, clearly not happy with the situation. "Levi
had the vehicle keys, so there doesn't seem to be much
doubt that he did it."

"Why?" She shoved the desk chair back. "That's
what kept me up half the night. What could Levi possibly have against us?"

"Emma was afraid she had the answer to that. It
seems the Zooks got worried that if the inn was successful, your grandmother might decide she wanted to use
the property they lease from her. She thinks Levi heard
them talking and misunderstood. Got some foolish idea
he was helping them. And Emma finally said that he
does get out at night sometimes."

Her throat tightened. "Poor Emma. It would be hard
for her to admit that."

"Well, your grandmother assured her the land is
theirs to use as long as they want it, and when I left they

were holding each other and crying, so I think they're going to be all right."

He shifted position, not looking at her. "You know, I have an offer to go out to the Zimmerman farm and work on a cabinetry job. I kept putting it off because of everything that's been going on here, but now that it's resolved, I should go."

"I see." She sensed he was saying more than the words indicated. "When will you leave?"

"This afternoon. It'll take a few days, so I suppose you'll be gone by the time I get back."

For a moment she couldn't speak. This was it, then. Cal was letting her know, in the nicest possible way, that he didn't want a relationship with her.

Well, that was for the best, wasn't it? They were committed to completely different values. This wasn't about the distance between Churchville and Philadelphia. It was a question of what they wanted from life. Since that couldn't be reconciled, it was better to make a clear break before anyone got hurt.

She managed to smile, forced herself to hold out her hand. "Thank you again for everything you've done to help us get under way. I'm sure I'll see you when I come back from time to time."

He nodded, holding her hand for a moment as if there was something else he wanted to say. Then he turned quickly and was gone.

She sank back in the chair. She'd been wrong about one thing. It was already too late to keep from getting hurt.

FIFTEEN

Barney whined, lifting his head from the library carpet to look at Andrea. He probably wondered why she was still at the computer when everyone else in the house was asleep. Over the past week, she'd gotten into the habit of keeping the dog downstairs with her after Grams went to bed, letting him out for one last time and then putting him into Grams's room when she went up.

"It's all right, boy." She leaned back in the desk chair, covering her eyes with her hands for a moment. The figures on the computer screen had begun to blur, particularly when she tried to compare them with the cramped writing in Grandfather's last couple of ledgers.

Maybe it would be better to take all of the financial records back to the city with her on Monday, so that she could go over them at her leisure. She'd begun to find discrepancies. It looked as if Grandfather had been failing more than she'd imagined in his final years.

She studied the portrait above the mantel, her grandfather's painted features staring back at her. Was that what happened? Had he really lost that sharp business sense of his and been too proud to admit it? She was startled to realize it hurt to think of him that way.

Aware of the dog whining again, she closed down the program and stacked the ledgers on the edge of the desk. "All right, Barney. You can go out, and then we'd both better get some sleep."

Barney, understanding the words *go out,* trotted toward the back door. When she opened it, he darted outside with a sharp woof.

She leaned against the door, trying not to look in the direction of the barn. Of Cal's empty apartment.

Working on the financial records had, for a few hours, absorbed her mind completely. She could get lost in the rows of figures as easily as other people got lost in a good book.

Now the pain came rushing back. Cal had shut the door on whatever might have been between them. She understood his reasons, but he could have given her some say in the matter. At least, he could have if he felt what she did.

Maybe she was wrong about that. Maybe those close moments between them, those kisses, had been merely attraction to him, with nothing more solid behind it.

Her mind fumbled with an unaccustomed prayer. *I'm trying to find my way back to You, Lord. For a while, I thought Cal was going to be part of that, but I was wrong. Still, no matter how much it hurts to lose him, knowing him has helped me look at things more clearly. Please, guide me to live the way You want.*

No lightning flashed. She didn't have a burst of insight. But peace seeped into her heart, easing the pain and giving her comfort.

Barney barked, the sound muted. Frowning, she stepped outside and called, "Barney! Here, boy!"

Nothing moved anywhere in the lighted area of the yard. He must have gone farther afield while she stood there lost in thought.

Everything looked perfectly peaceful, but somewhere beyond the fringe of outbuildings, the dog yipped.

She reached back inside to slip the flashlight off its hook. She'd have to get him—if she went up to bed without him, Grams would have a fit. And he'd probably wake the house with his barking.

At least, with Levi in the hospital, she didn't have to worry about encountering any prowlers. Poor Levi. Would charges be brought against him? Surely not, if Grams had anything to say about it.

She crossed to the toolshed, shining the light around. Beyond the range of the security lights it was pitch-black, the sliver of a new moon providing little illumination.

She called again, her voice sharp. This time the answer was a whining cry that sounded distressed, and her fingers tightened on the flashlight. Was Barney hurt? Trapped in some way? She hurried toward the sound, behind the row of outbuildings, into the blackness.

Yards ahead of her, across the overgrown lane, loomed the dark bulk of the old barn. A shiver went down her spine. The sound seemed to be coming from there.

The building had been kept in repair, but it hadn't been used for anything in years. Still, there might be something that Barney's collar could have become hooked on.

That must be it.

She trotted toward the earthen ramp to the upper level, flicking the flashlight around as she went, hoping she wouldn't spot any night creatures larger than a mouse. But the dog's presence had probably frightened away any other animals.

One of the big double doors stood ajar just enough for Barney to get through. She'd have to see that it was secured—something else to add to her to-do list. They couldn't have inn guests wandering around where they might get hurt.

She entered, swinging the light. The space was empty, an oil mark on the floor mute testimony to the farm vehicle that had once been parked there. Grandfather must have had the barn cleared out when it was no longer in use.

Her flashlight beam picked up a small door opposite the entrance. The dog's now-frantic barking came from there.

She hurried across the dusty floorboards and grabbed the door, yanking it open. A foul, metallic aroma rushed out at her. Memory stirred. They'd kept fertilizers and pesticides in here long ago. Her light bounced off floor-to-ceiling shelves, still laden with rusty cans. The place looked like a toxic waste dump. Her grandfather's care of the building hadn't extended to clearing this out, apparently.

Barney's eyes shone in the light, and he wiggled with impatience. "Barney." She was embarrassed at the slight tremor in her voice, even though there was no one but the dog to hear. "What happened, baby? Are you stuck?"

Sure enough, the dog's collar was caught in the prongs of an old harrow that lay on the floor. She hurried to kneel beside him. When she patted him, she had to try to quiet his excited leaps and attempts to lick her face.

"Hold still, you silly thing. I can't release you when you're doing that." She put the flashlight down, fumbling with the collar, the dog's jumps nearly knocking her over. The flashlight rolled, illuminating what lay in the corner.

Nick Bendick. Uncle Nick. He sprawled against the wall, unconscious. Alive? Her heart seemed to stop.

"Uncle Nick?" She hurried to him, dropping to her knees next to the inert form.

She groped for his wrist, breathing again when she felt a pulse—weak, but at least he was alive. She grabbed the flashlight, trying to focus with hands that were shaking. It looked as if he'd stumbled on the harrow, hitting his head against the wall. But what on earth was he doing here?

The circle of light wavered, and she forced herself to steady it. It touched Nick's hand, lying lax on the barn floor. Her breath caught, and the world seemed to spin.

In Nick's hand was a dog leash, next to it a torn paper bag, dog biscuits spilling from it.

She couldn't seem to move. Barney hadn't gotten tangled up on his own. Nick had been waiting, knowing she always let the dog out the last thing at night. Had trapped Barney, apparently intending to use him to lure her here.

Her mind struggled to the obvious conclusion. The financial records. Anger swept through her. This was about her interest in the financial records. Grandfather hadn't been losing his touch. Nick had been cheating him.

She had to get help. Run to the house, call the paramedics and the police, let them sort it out. She hurried back to the dog, struggled with the collar for another moment, and finally got it free.

Uncle Nick. It was impossible to believe. Could he really have intended to hurt her? Surely he'd never hurt anyone in his life.

Except Levi. Her mind seemed to leap from one understanding to another. Levi, lying on the floor with the keys planted next to him. How much of what had been happening had been caused by Nick's frantic efforts to keep her from looking into the financial records? He must have realized she was the one person who would understand what he'd done.

The authorities would figure it out. Barney beside her, she hurried toward the door. Cool night air hit her like a slap in the face. Get help. That was all she could do now.

She darted toward the distant house, the circle of light bouncing ahead of her, and Barney woofed at the unexpected excitement. If Grams heard him, came out—well, she'd have to know the truth about the man she'd trusted soon, in any event.

If Cal were at the barn, she'd call on him for help. But he wasn't. He'd left. Ridiculous, to feel that she needed him.

She rounded the corner of the toolshed and flew straight into someone.

She stumbled back, gasping. The security light showed her Betty, of all people. Another surprise in a night of surprises. She grasped the woman's arm.

"You have to help me. It's Nick—he's hurt. He—"

"I'll help."

Betty patted her reassuringly with one hand. The other lifted something. Light reflected from a long, silvery shaft. It swung down, pain exploded in her head, and the ground came up to meet her.

Andrea struggled to open her eyes, but her head spun and ached. She'd just lie here another minute…

Then consciousness came rolling back. Nick. And Betty. Betty had hit her with a golf club. Impossible, but it had happened. Nick and Betty must be doing this together.

A warm, furry body next to her, a rough wet tongue washing her face. "Barney," she whispered, coughing on the word.

She moved, aware of hard wooden boards beneath her, of the acrid smell that made her want to gag. She was back in the tiny storage room in the old barn. Barney was with her.

Something hard poked into her ribs. She rolled,

feeling for it, and pulled out the flashlight. Fumbled for the switch, thinking if she had to stay in the dark another instant she'd start screaming...

The light came on. Maybe this was worse. She could see the tall shelves on either side of her, enclosing her with their load of poison. She sucked in a breath and was instantly sorry when the air burned her throat.

Then she saw what still lay against the wall. Nick.

Her mind spun.

Get out. She had to get out. She stumbled to the door, groping for the handle. Locked. Incredibly, Betty had locked her in here. Betty. How could she even have gotten her here? It was impossible.

Then she identified the sound that rumbled from beyond the door. A car's engine. Betty must have driven up the overgrown lane behind the outbuildings and hauled her in here.

She pounded on the door. "Betty! Let me out of here. You can't get away with this."

"Can't I?" Betty's voice was muffled by the thick door, but she must be standing close to it on the other side. "I think I can. You've always underestimated me, all of you. My plans have been made for a long time, my money safely salted away under another name. I knew Nick would break down at some point. He always had such a soft spot for your grandmother."

She sounded like an indulgent mother, admitting a failing in her child.

"You were stealing from the firm." Hard to think it through, with the fumes fogging her brain. "But Nick— was he in it with you? Is that what this was all about?"

"Nick had a little gambling problem, you see. Borrowed some money from the accounts. He wasn't very good at it. Your grandfather would have found him out in a week if it hadn't been for me." There was a trace of pride in her voice.

"Betty, think about what you're doing." She forced herself to be calm. Rational. One of them should be. "Just let me out, and we'll go to the police together. I'll get you a lawyer—"

Betty chuckled. "Dear Andrea, always so sure you know what's best. I have no intention of going to the police. You and Nick are going to have an unfortunate accident, and I'm going to be far away by the time it's sorted out and they start to look for me."

"Accident..." She tried to move, but her muscles didn't obey. She could lie down, just rest for a moment; it would be all right....

Shock sent her upright. Her mental fog wasn't just from the closed room and the cans of chemicals. The car was running because Betty was pumping carbon monoxide into the room.

She dropped to her knees, fingers fumbling along the bottom of the door. Yes, there was the mouth of a hose, thrust under the corner of the door.

Please, Lord, please, Lord, help me know what to do. If I can just block it...

She swung the light around, picking up an old feed sack shoved onto a shelf. Grab it, twist a piece small enough to fit into the hose, stuff it in, coughing and choking, pray it blocked enough to give them a few more precious moments to live....

A few moments. Not enough. No one would look for her until morning, probably. How long would it take until they searched here?

She slumped back, trying to force her numbed wits to move. The walls were closing in. She couldn't stop them, and she felt the familiar panic, blurred by her fogged mind, but there, creeping in, loosening her control.

Father, help me hold on. If I panic, I'll die. Forgive me for drifting away from You. Hold me in Your hands, living or dying.

Hands. Hands reaching out to her, pulling her free. She shook her head, knowing it was a memory, but a memory of what?

It wouldn't come. Think. What else could she do?

Noises outside the door. A car door opening and closing. The car driving away. Betty was gone.

She was still alive, and so was Nick from what she could tell. But not for long unless she could think of something. She swung the light around. Metal shone for an instant on the shelf—she reached, hand closing on a bar about the size of a tire iron.

Excitement flooded her, clearing her mind. If she could get the door open...

But a moment's effort showed her that was impossible. The door was solid, resisting her feeble efforts to open it.

Think. Think. If you can't get out, maybe you can get air in. The wall behind her was solid stone, the end wall of the barn. Nothing there, but the wall to her right must be an outside wall.

She crawled over to it, dragging the bar. Barney, whimpering a little, struggled to her side. Was it her imagination, or was the air a little better here? The dog seemed to think so. He put his nose at the base of the wall, right where the siding boards came down to meet the floor.

Nick. She crawled back to him, grabbed his arms, and dragged him toward the wall. No time now to worry that she was injuring him further. If she didn't get them some air, they would die.

Adrenaline pulsing, she ran her hand along the joint, feeling the slightest crack between the boards. Big enough to wedge the bar in? Her fingers seemed to have grown stupid along with her brain. It took three tries before she forced the bar in.

Wiggle it, shove it, find something to hit it with—but there she ran out of luck. There was nothing loose in the room sturdy enough to hit the bar. She'd have to keep wiggling it, trying to force it through to the outside, but her mind was fogging again.

Ironic. She'd filled up the slight crack with the pry bar, cutting off whatever air might come through.

Give me strength, Lord. Help me. I know You're here with me. I know whatever You intend is right. But I can't stop trying, can't stop fighting....

"To everything there is a season, and a time for every purpose under Heaven. A time to live and a time to die..."

Barney slumped to the floor. Poor boy. He'd go first. She and Nick were bigger, so they'd last longer. Push, keep pushing, a little farther...

"A little farther, Drea." Her grandfather's voice. He

was the only one who'd ever called her that. "Just a little farther. Don't stop now. Another inch, and you'll reach my hands."

Another inch. A vague dream of Grandfather's strong hands, tight on hers, lifting her out into the cool air, holding her close. Safe. She'd always been safe with him.

Safe in God's hands. Living or dying...

Another inch. She pushed the bar, felt the resistance give way as it slid through. Befuddled. Taking a moment to realize she had to pull the bar back out.

Feel the cool air on her face, rushing in through the hole she'd made. Drinking in long gasps of it. Drag Nick's limp form, then Barney, up to the opening, feeling the dog stir.

But tired. So tired. She slumped down, head on Barney's fur.

SIXTEEN

Cal eased off on the accelerator when he hit the outskirts of Churchville. He was making a fool of himself, rushing back at this hour, but the urge to see Andrea again, to clear the air between them, had been too strong to ignore.

He'd tried hiding from life, and it hadn't worked. He couldn't hide. Life kept finding him.

And beneath that urge to see Andrea had been something he couldn't explain, a sense that all was not right. An urgent feeling that he was needed.

Well, he was here, and how he'd explain arriving at this late hour, he didn't know. They'd all be asleep, probably, and he'd have to wait until morning to see Andrea anyway.

But as he turned into the drive at the inn, he saw the glow of lights in the library. It had to be Andrea, sitting up late at the computer. Relief flooded through him, making him realize just how tense he'd been.

A glimpse of movement drew his attention. From beyond the outbuildings, a dark car spurted out, hit the winding country road and raced away.

Cal jammed on the brakes and slid out, leaving the

motor running, all his instincts crying out. That was wrong, very wrong. He ran toward the back door, and the minute he saw it, he knew his instincts were on target. The door stood open, light pooling out onto the patio, and no one was there.

His feet thudded across the patio. None of them would go off and leave the door standing open at this hour. He bolted inside and ran for the library. Lights on, computer on, desk chair pushed back. It looked as if Andrea had just walked away.

Some rational part of his mind kept insisting that there could be a logical explanation, but he didn't believe it. Rachel—Rachel was sleeping on this floor now, in the little room off the kitchen.

He saw the light go on as he ran to it. He was probably scaring her to death.

"Rachel, it's Cal. Is Andrea with you?"

"No. What's happening?" Fear laced her voice.

He flung open the door. Rachel sat up in bed, pulling a robe around her.

"The back door is standing open, and I can't find Andrea."

"If she took the dog out—"

He felt as if he'd been doused with cold water. "That must be it. Sorry. I'll just check."

Logical explanation, see? But the fear drove him back out to the patio. "Andrea! Andrea, are you out here?"

A light went on overhead, and he heard footsteps on the stairs. Katherine. She hurried toward him.

"Cal, what are you doing back? Why are you calling for Andrea?"

"Is she upstairs?"

"No." She glanced toward the library and paled. "She and Barney were still down here. She must have taken him out. But why didn't she hear you call?"

"I'll look for her. Where's a flashlight?"

She pulled a drawer open and thrust a heavy torch into his hand. "I'm calling the police."

He jerked a nod and hurried out the door. Better a false alarm than a tragedy. He'd never been one to go on instinct, but this sense was stronger than he'd ever experienced.

Is it You, Lord? If it is, help me to listen. Show me where to go. Please, keep her safe.

He ran across the lawn toward the outbuildings. The car that had no possible reason for being there—it had come from behind the outbuildings. He swung the light around.

"Andrea! Where are you?"

Nothing. The buildings were dark and silent, the security lights reflecting from them, mocking him. They hadn't kept Andrea safe.

And the dog—the dog must be with her. "Barney!" he yelled. "Here, boy. Barney!"

Not even an answering woof. He paused by the tool-shed, the urgency pounding along his veins like a power in his blood, telling him to hurry, hurry. But where?

Lord, help me. If this is from You, help me.

He took a breath. Think. The car came down the disused lane behind the outbuildings—the lane that led only to the old barn. He ran, heart thudding in his ears. Behind him, from the house, the bell began clanging insistently. Katherine, trying to rouse the Zook family to come and help.

The circle of light bounced. He rounded the corner, saw the barn doors, and knew the instinct that drove him was right. Both doors stood open, and the grass leading to them was bent down from the passage of a car.

He thudded inside. A car had been in here—he could smell the fumes. Strong, too strong. He swung the light around. Empty, nothing…

The light flashed on a door—solid as the barn, the old-fashioned latch dropped down into its pocket, securing it. He ran toward it, stumbling on a length of hose, righting himself, reaching the door.

Flung it open and staggered back from the fumes. Andrea. He took a deep breath and threw himself through the door. Woman and dog lay together against the outer wall. Another figure—a man. Bendick. Still, too still.

He grabbed Andrea, stumbled back out, through the barn, out into the cold night air. Think, remember your CPR training, but even as he thought it she coughed, choked and gasped in a gulp of air.

Tears filled his eyes. *Please, God, please, God.* He knelt in the damp grass, holding her against him. "Andrea, wake up. Say something. Breathe."

She stirred, murmured something, then sank limply against him. But she was breathing. Her eyelids fluttered.

"I've found her!" he shouted at the top of his lungs. "Call the paramedics." Poor Katherine must be terrified, but he couldn't do anything else. He'd have to go back in for Bendick….

Lights bobbing toward him—Eli, his son and the

oldest grandson with him, running with trousers pulled on over nightshirts.

"In the barn, the back room. Bendick and the dog. Mind the fumes." Samuel nodded and pelted into the barn with the boy, while Eli knelt beside him.

"Will she be all right, then?"

"She's breathing." He looked at the older man, not ashamed of the tears that spilled over. "She's alive."

"Thank the Lord," Eli said.

The wail of a siren split the night.

Yes, thank You, Father. Thank You.

Andrea toyed with the piece of dry toast that was all she thought she could get down. They sat around the breakfast table in various stages of exhaustion. Emma kept pressing food on people, as if that were the only cure for the night they'd been through.

Since she'd missed most of it, either through being unconscious or at the hospital, she tried to concentrate on what Chief Burkhalter was saying, but her gaze kept straying to Cal.

His face was drawn, the skin pulled tight against the bone, as if he'd been in battle and wasn't sure it was over. She'd had no chance to talk with him alone, and still didn't know what had brought him back. She only knew he'd come in time to save her. That was enough.

Barney padded around the table from Grams to her, sighed, and thudded heavily to the floor next to her, as if he'd decided that she needed his protection.

"...caught up with the woman the other side of Harrisburg," Burkhalter was saying. "She tried to bluff it out. Might have gotten away if Burke hadn't gotten to you in time." He eyed her soberly. "Just glad you're okay."

She nodded, not sure she trusted herself to speak. The memory was too fresh.

"I don't understand." Grams seemed to have aged overnight. "I'd believe anything of Betty, but Nick— we've known him and trusted him for thirty years."

"Are they talking?" Cal asked.

Burkhalter shrugged. "The woman clammed up tight and asked for a lawyer. Bendick is still in the hospital, but he's babbling like Conestoga Creek." He turned to Grams. "Might make you feel a little better to know that apparently Bendick never intended to steal from the company. He had gambling losses he was ashamed to admit to your husband, took money to pay them off intending to replace it, he says, but the secretary found out and started blackmailing him. I imagine a thorough look into the books will prove she helped herself to quite a bit. Whether you'll ever get it back again is another question. The lawyers will have to sort that out."

"I still don't understand," Rachel said. "What was the point of all of the tricks they pulled? Was that Uncle Nick or Betty?"

"According to Bendick, they figured Andrea was the one person who might make sense of their doctored records, especially if she got hold of her grandfather's ledgers. The secretary was pulling the strings, blackmailing him to try and scare Andrea away. He claims he couldn't take it anymore, was coming here to tell you the truth when she attacked him."

The timing suddenly made sense. "I had the ledgers on my desk in the afternoon, when Betty stopped in. She must have thought I was on to them."

"We found the ledgers in her car," Burkhalter said. "Looks like they had some hope of locating them before you did. And he thought if Mrs. Unger gave up the idea of the inn, you'd go back to the city and leave things alone."

"Levi saw him." Emma spoke unexpectedly, her hands holding tight to the back of Grams's chair. "He finally told us. He saw Mr. Bendick here when he shouldn't of been. He wanted to tell Andrea, but he was too shy. Mr. Bendick said to meet him in Cal's place, so he could explain. Instead he pushed him."

"Levi—he was trying to tell me that night when he stood outside the house. And he followed me when I left the farm."

Emma nodded. "He meant to help. He didn't know how."

It was all starting to fall into place. "What about Rachel, the hit-and-run? Did they do that?"

"Bendick claims not," Burkhalter said. "We'll keep looking, but we may never know the truth about that."

Grams reached up to clasp Emma's hand. "At least Levi and Rachel are going to be all right."

"And Ms. Hampton," Burkhalter added. "The secretary hoped we'd think Bendick was guilty, at least long enough to let her get away." He shifted his gaze to Cal. "What made you come back, Burke? Did you suspect it was something to do with the books?"

Her breath stopped. *Why, Cal? How did you know?*

"No, not at all." He looked as if he were blaming himself. "I just…" He hesitated. "I just had a feeling."

Grams glanced at the clock and got to her feet. "Goodness, we'll be having guests here before you know it. We have to get ready." She bustled around the table, making shooing motions with her hands. "Andrea, you go and rest before you fall over. We'll take care of everything. Go on now."

People began to scatter. If Cal intended to tell her anything, it would have to wait.

The final guests left on Monday afternoon, heaping delighted praise on Three Sisters Inn. Andrea looked at Grams and Rachel. They wore grins just as goofy as hers probably was.

"We actually did it," she said. "I'm not sure I believed it would work."

"I did." Rachel patted her arm. "Thanks to you, and Grams, and Emma, and Nancy, and everyone else who helped out."

"They all said they'd be back." Grams sounded a little surprised. "Two couples have already booked for a second visit."

"You know, Grams, if you're able to recover the money Betty stole, you might not have to run the inn." She was fairly certain she knew the answer to that, but they may as well get it out in the open.

Grams looked astonished. "Not run the inn? Of course we will. This is the most fun I've had in years."

Andrea hugged her. It looked as if she'd been wrong

about a lot of things, but this was one time when she didn't mind that.

Grams patted her. "You should go and rest. You both should."

"Sounds good." Rachel stifled a yawn.

"I think I'll go out back and get some fresh air first." Andrea whistled to Barney, who scurried to her side. She patted his head. "You're my self-appointed watchdog, aren't you?" So maybe he wasn't the brightest dog in the world, but he was loyal.

Afternoon sun slanted across the lawn, filtering through the trees to touch the brilliant colors of the flowers. The sandstone patio wall glowed golden. Cal sat, just where she thought she might find him.

The dog padded quietly at her heels as she stepped off the patio and went to sit beside him.

He gave her a questioning look. "You're not turned off by the view out here after what happened to you?"

That was a nice, safe way to start what they had to say to each other. "It's still beautiful." She managed to look at the dark bulk of the old barn where it lifted above the outbuildings. "I guess there's something about nearly dying that makes you appreciate life."

"I should have been here," he said abruptly, emotion roughening his voice. "I shouldn't have left until I was sure everything was all right."

Sorrow deepened. It would have been better if he'd said he shouldn't have left at all, but he hadn't. She'd have to accept that.

"You came back in time, that's all that counts." It

took an effort to keep her voice even. "What made you come back, Cal? I need to know."

He touched her hand lightly, and that touch seemed to reverberate through her. "I kept thinking I'd been unfair, leaving the way I did without talking to you. I tried telling myself I'd done it for the best, but I wasn't very convincing." He looked at her then. "I'm sorry."

She nodded, trying to dispel the lump in her throat. "That's why you came back last night? Because you'd been wrong to leave without talking to me?"

"Not exactly." His brow furrowed. "I don't know if I can explain. I just felt an overwhelming pressure to come, not to wait for morning, not to delay, just to come." His fingers wrapped around hers. "I think God was giving me the push I needed. That's the only explanation I have."

"It's all you need." The feelings she'd had when she was trapped came flooding back—the assurance of God's presence, the half-remembered dream about Grandfather. "Remember when you asked me what brought on my claustrophobia?"

He looked startled by the change of subject, but nodded.

"I found out. Some of it I remembered, some Grams told me. When I was five, I fell into an abandoned well behind the old barn."

"That would certainly do it."

She nodded. "Grandfather was out in the field with Eli and some of the men. They heard me cry. My grandfather had the men hold his legs and lower him down so that I could reach his hands. He pulled me out."

"And you didn't remember it?"

"No. I asked Grams why they didn't tell me, but apparently they thought it was better forgotten. Last night—last night I remembered, some of it at least. When I was digging the airhole, I could feel God's presence with me. Somehow I'd lost that certainty of His presence, but now it's back. And I remembered my grandfather's voice, telling me to reach farther so I could take his hand. It kept me going."

Cal held her hand between his palms, and his touch comforted her. "You feel differently about your grandfather than you did when you came."

She nodded, wanting to articulate it. He needed to understand how she'd changed. "I can see him more clearly now, and look at the situation like an adult instead of a child. He was a strong, stubborn, fallible human being, not a superhero. He loved and he made mistakes, like we all do. But the loving—that was the important part."

"I'm glad," he said simply.

She turned to face him. "Understanding that made me see that I want things to be straight between us. No long silences or things left unsaid."

"That's asking a lot. I'm not sure I'm brave enough for that."

"I think you are." She had to give him the choice. Either they could take the risk of loving each other, or he could go back to hiding from the world in his safe, peaceful sanctuary.

He looked down at their clasped hands. "You know why I left. I'd started to care about you too much. I knew the kind of life you want, and I couldn't ask you to change. It seemed better—safer, I guess—if we parted before it became too difficult." The corner of his lips curled slightly. "I was wrong. It was more than difficult. It was impossible. Andrea, I know that hiding isn't the answer for me. I choose this life because it's right for me, but I don't want it to come between us."

Something lifted inside her, and she wanted to laugh. They'd been so foolish, trying to protect themselves from falling in love. God had known better than they had.

"Funny thing about that." She couldn't help the lilt to her voice. "Being here with family again, seeing how unreasonable my boss is and how cutthroat my colleagues, made me take a serious look at what I want out of life. Maybe that security I was looking for doesn't mean I have to have the biggest office, or make the most money."

He was looking at her with so much love shining in his eyes that she didn't know whether she should laugh or cry.

"I was thinking I might start a little bookkeeping business of my own, where I could be my own boss. You know any small towns that might need a business like that?"

He slid his arm around her and drew her close. "I think we might be able to find the right place. And I know a carpenter who'll give you a good price on office furniture."

She leaned into him, feeling his strength, knowing his character and his faith. She'd been looking for security in the wrong place, just as Cal had been looking for peace in the wrong place. God was calling them to love and to dare, not to hide and be safe.

She lifted her face, meeting his lips, and knew this time she was home to stay.

* * * * *

Watch for Marta Perry's next novel,
A CHRISTMAS TO DIE FOR,
the second story in the exciting new miniseries
The Three Sisters Inn.
Danger awaits the Hampton sisters
in quiet Amish Country.
On sale November 2007 from
Steeple Hill Love Inspired Suspense

Dear Reader,

Thank you for picking up this first story in THE THREE SISTERS INN series. With this series I come back to my beautiful rural Pennsylvania and the good, neighborly people who live here, especially that unique group, the Amish.

I am indebted to Chris and Jim, proprietors of the lovely and welcoming Churchtown Inn Bed & Breakfast, for giving me an inside look at their operation and answering my questions. But please don't think that any of the dangerous doings in my story happened there—they are all the product of my own imagination!

I hope you'll let me know how you felt about the story. I've put together a little collection of Pennsylvania Dutch recipes that I'd be happy to share with you—some from my own family, some from friends. You can write to me at Steeple Hill Books, 233 Broadway, Suite 1001, New York, NY 10279; e-mail me at marta@martaperry.com; or visit me on the Web at www.martaperry.com.

Blessings,

Marta Perry

QUESTIONS FOR DISCUSSION

1. Can you understand the need for security that drives Andrea into being something of a workaholic? Have you ever felt that financial security is the most important thing in life?

2. Cal seeks isolation as a way of dealing with the terrible mistake he made. Do you sympathize with his feelings, even if you may not approve of his reactions?

3. Andrea has a close relationship with her sister, even though they no longer live together closely. Do you have a sister or a woman friend with whom you have the sort of relationship that isn't damaged by distance?

4. The struggle to heal the wounds of the past is central to this story. Have you ever gone through a similar struggle? What helped you the most?

5. Andrea begins to see that being called back home is part of being called back to God. Have you ever felt that God has led you to a particular place or situation?

6. Andrea finds comfort and insight through the Sunlight and Shadow quilt and the Scripture

passages she associates with it. Has an object ever provided similar comfort and insight to you?

7. Cal finds healing in the people he meets in his new home and in making furniture. Is there an art or craft in which you can find pleasure and relief from daily tensions?

8. In the scriptural theme, we see reflected the passages of life. What particular incidents in your life are brought to mind by this verse?

9. Most Old Order Amish believe that by living separate from the world, they can serve God more clearly. Do you understand their attitude, even if you don't share it?

10. Have you ever felt that technological advances like cell phones and computers are detracting from your family time or your religious life? If so, how do you deal with that?

REQUEST YOUR FREE BOOKS!
2 FREE RIVETING INSPIRATIONAL NOVELS
PLUS 2 FREE MYSTERY GIFTS

Love Inspired®
SUSPENSE

YES! Please send me 2 FREE Love Inspired® Suspense novels and my 2 FREE mystery gifts. After receiving them, if I don't wish to receive any more books, I can return the shipping statement marked "cancel." If I don't cancel, I will receive 4 brand-new novels every month and be billed just $3.99 per book in the U.S. or $4.74 per book in Canada, plus 25¢ shipping and handling per book and applicable taxes, if any*. That's a savings of 20% off the cover price! I understand that accepting the 2 free books and gifts places me under no obligation to buy anything. I can always return a shipment and cancel at any time. Even if I never buy another book from Steeple Hill, the two free books and gifts are mine to keep forever.

123 IDN EL5H   323 IDN ELQH

Name	(PLEASE PRINT)	
Address		Apt. #
City	State/Prov.	Zip/Postal Code

Signature (if under 18, a parent or guardian must sign)

Order online at www.LoveInspiredSuspense.com

Or mail to Steeple Hill Reader Service™:

IN U.S.A.: P.O. Box 1867, Buffalo, NY 14240-1867
IN CANADA: P.O. Box 609, Fort Erie, Ontario L2A 5X3

Not valid to current Love Inspired Suspense subscribers.

Want to try two free books from another series?
Call 1-800-873-8635 or visit www.morefreebooks.com

* Terms and prices subject to change without notice. NY residents add applicable sales tax. Canadian residents will be charged applicable provincial taxes and GST. This offer is limited to one order per household. All orders subject to approval. Credit or debit balances in a customer's account(s) may be offset by any other outstanding balance owed by or to the customer. Please allow 4 to 6 weeks for delivery.

Your Privacy: Steeple Hill is committed to protecting your privacy. Our Privacy Policy is available online at www.eHarlequin.com or upon request from the Reader Service. From time to time we make our lists of customers available to reputable firms who may have a product or service of interest to you. If you would prefer we not share your name and address, please check here. ☐

LISUS07

Love Inspired®

Celebrate Love Inspired's 10th anniversary with top authors and great stories all year long!

A Mommy in Mind
by Arlene Jones

A Tiny Blessings Tale

Reporter Lori Sumner's adoption of a little girl was nearly complete when the baby's teenage mother changed her mind. And even if it meant being pitted against handsome attorney Ramon Estes, Lori was determined to fight for her child!

Steeple Hill®

Available September wherever you buy books.

Love Inspired® SUSPENSE

TITLES AVAILABLE NEXT MONTH

Don't miss these four stories in September

GONE TO GLORY by Ron and Janet Benrey
Cozy Mystery
Fraud was all in a day's work for savvy insurance investigator
Lori Dorsett. But her city smarts needed some bolstering
from bachelor pastor Daniel Hartman to locate a missing
million dollars...and the real murderer lurking among the
members of Glory Community Church.

SECRET AGENT MINISTER by Lenora Worth
The minister of Lydia Cantrell's dreams had another calling–
Pastor Malone was a secret agent, a dynamic rescuer of
missionaries in danger. Yet would his skill be enough to save
them from the danger that lurked far too close to home?

TO TRUST A STRANGER by Lynn Bulock
Nobody believed Jessie Barker's childhood tale: her mother
had survived their family's fiery car crash. Now, with her
sister lying injured after a mysterious attack, Jessie would
need stalwart deputy Steve Gardner to solve the bizarre
mystery her life had become....

DESPERATE RESCUE by Barbara Phinney
Leaving meant paying a price. When Kaylee Campbell
escaped the cult, leader Noah Nash murdered her sister. And
when his brother, looking very much like Noah, appeared on
her doorstep, would her faith permit her to believe her safety
rested in his hands?